For Michael, who brings the sunshine to my life
For Holly, my granddaughter, with much love
For Claire, that she might understand

Foreword

It was never my intention to commit my thoughts and feelings to paper, let alone write a book.

For some time after my search for Claire had concluded, I had great difficulty in talking about it at all. Gradually I began to share my thoughts and feelings with Michael, my husband, and later on, with Rory, my son. After some time, I began to confide in close friends and relations.

When I *did* open up to people, the reaction was so positive that I began to realise that perhaps to share my story with a wider audience might be of interest and of use to others. It was with the encouragement of my GP, Jon Chappell, that I finally decided to write a book about it.

In truth, however, I wrote this book in the first place for myself, in an effort to come to some understanding of all that had happened over the years. My search for Claire was my bid for personal wholeness, though I doubt if I really understood this at the time. Now I feel that my story might in some way be helpful to other women of my generation—or beyond—who have experienced similar suffering.

This story, or extract from my life, is written, I hope, without any sense of recrimination or bitterness, as I feel I have long since realised the futility of such destructive emotions.

Fionnuala Batts

PART ONE

CHAPTER ONE

I was a Christmas baby, born in Dublin in 1943, the second surviving child of my family. I arrived on a crisp, frosty day around twelve noon. I did not make my entry into the world until my brother, Michael, was five years old, so I must have been wanted and very much cherished. I can recall, as a young child, being cosseted by my mother, who fretted over my every cough and sneeze.

When I was about twelve months old my parents moved to a small town near the east coast. My father took up a post as principal in a rural school about four miles from the town. In the forties and early fifties he would cycle to school each day, rain, snow or sunshine. I can still see him in my mind's eye as he set out each morning, complete with waterproof cape. Most days he would return home around four o'clock, weary after his day's work. There were times, however, when he was not so tired and if he was in a good mood, he would take me, as a great treat, for a spin down the road on his big black bike.

In the fifties all that changed, as my father was then

able to buy a second-hand car. What excitement it caused! It was an old Austin and he learned to drive it on the country roads outside the town. There was no driving test in those days. Cars were few and far between and anyone who had one tended to take very good care of it. Quite often, on a summer Sunday afternoon, we would all pile into the car and take a trip to the beach, some forty miles from our home.

Both my brother and I went to local schools. I was educated by the nuns, my brother attended the Christian Brothers. I think we were both conscious of growing up in a small town where our father was highly respected and had a place on many of the local committees, as well as being involved in church work. As was the custom in rural Ireland and small towns, we were referred to as "the master's children." Even though we were pleased to be recognised in the small community, this nevertheless entailed certain drawbacks. For instance, it was taken for granted that we both came equipped with high intelligence and we were expected to excel at everything. We got little credit for our achievements: usually someone would just remark, "Well, and sure why wouldn't you? Isn't your daddy the master?"

My mother was a quiet, retiring woman and was content to look after her husband and family. She was a great cook and home-maker, happy in the shadow of my father's popularity.

When we were young Sundays were great days, with a special dinner, an outing of some sort—to the beach or the cinema—in the afternoon and cake for supper. First Communion and Confirmation days were highlights in every child's life, and summer holidays were very enjoyable occasions for us.

My parents usually managed to take us away for a holiday and they loved to visit Howth, then a small, sleepy seaside town on the outskirts of Dublin. The family took a cottage there for the month of August. In the late forties and early fifties we usually travelled there by train. I have vivid memories of a large, strong brown trunk occupying quite a bit of space on the sitting-room floor during the last days of July, as we prepared for departure. We would get up early on the morning of the journey and I can still see the big black engine with smoke billowing out of the high-domed chimney, and smell the fumes as if it were yesterday. When we arrived at Amiens Street Station in Dublin we had to catch another train to Howth Station and from there we would get a taxi to the cottage, which was in a place called "The Haggard." We would settle in very quickly, eat a hurried meal, and if the weather was warm, in no time at all get to the beach to paddle in the sea along with many other children. The holiday would pass in the usual pleasurable way, with visits to the local shops, games, and deep sleeps at night.

Not all the holiday memories, however, are idyllic for me. I recall some summers when I was about five or six years old, when my parents would meet up with friends, some former teaching colleagues of my father's from his days in Dublin. This happened specially at weekends when a lot of Dubliners travelled out of the city to get some sea air. I did not particularly look forward to such times and I recall feeling apprehensive when I was told that certain visitors would be coming to the house to see us. These people were long-standing friends of my parents and some years older than them, and we referred to them as Uncle Jim and Auntie Lou.

On a few occasions they stayed with us at the cottage and I developed an intense mistrust of Uncle Jim. We would all have tea together and then my parents would go for a walk on Howth Head as soon as the washing-up was done and Michael and I were sent off to bed. Michael always had a great supply of comics and once he became involved in some story from *Our Boys*, would scarcely notice if the house went on fire. As he got older he was sometimes allowed to play outside with neighbours' children and it was then that Uncle Jim would offer to keep an eye on me to allow my parents the freedom to enjoy their evening stroll. Aunt Lou frequently went along with them, so I was left alone in the house with Uncle Jim. I was tucked up in bed with my favourite doll, Mary Jane. My bedroom door was usually left slightly ajar so that I would not feel too alone. Uncle Jim often listened to the wireless and would from time to time pop into my bedroom to see if I was asleep. Sometimes he would sit on the side of my bed and read me a story. This was enjoyable until he began to slip into bed beside me, pressing himself tightly to me and breathing heavily, his hands touching my genitals. After a while he would stroke my head and kiss me on the cheek, before slipping quietly out of the room and closing the door. He would often bring me presents and referred to me as his "special little girl."

I was very upset by his behaviour, and knew even at this tender age that something was wrong. I felt, however, that it ought not be spoken of in case I would in some way be blamed. My father appeared to have a very high regard for this Uncle Jim and was totally ignorant of his betrayal of trust. I was always happy to see the back of these particular visitors and as I grew older I became adept at keeping out of Uncle Jim's way, until he must have concluded that it was wiser to leave me alone.

I feel today that the saddest aspect of this incident was my inability to inform my parents. I think they would have believed me and done something about it. The amount of psychological damage done to a child like me is difficult to measure, but there is now no doubt in my mind that these experiences had a catastrophic effect on my life and played no small part in my future unhappiness. A child who has been sexually abused is left with feelings of guilt and a great lack of self-esteem, and becomes secretive, untrusting and insecure. I can see this now only with hindsight, having spent considerable time in later years in psychotherapy, trying to undo some of the damage this man caused me.

Growing up in a small rural town in Ireland in the fifties and sixties was like living in a large extended family. From the time you got up in the morning until the time you went to bed at night you were in a goldfish bowl. Everything was known about the local families' breed, seed and generation. People like ourselves who came to live in a small town were still regarded as "blow-ins" after nearly twenty years but were regarded with great interest and curiosity nonetheless.

I went to the local convent school for the first few

years of my secondary education and it was here that I was first introduced to drama: I can remember performing in a play in Irish for the local Feis. The staff, like that of most Irish schools at the time, was almost entirely composed of nuns. I was regarded by my father as being of "good average" intelligence, and he therefore expected me to do well in my studies. My brother Michael was much more inclined to be studious than I was: I tended rather to get into hot water with my teachers. I did manage to do well in my Intermediate Certificate, despite gloomy predictions from the convent. My father then decided that it would be a good idea to send me off to boarding school for the last two years of secondary education, so that pressure could be put on me to knuckle down to work. My mother frequently reminded me that there was no family business or farm for me to inherit, so my Leaving Certificate results would be all-important. St Mary's College, Arklow, was the school chosen for me.

In the main, I disliked being at boarding school, although it probably did me good. It was difficult, at sixteen years of age, to make new friends in a class where friendships had been well established for the previous four years. But life became tolerable and I settled into the routine. We had a film—usually censored—on Sunday evening and my school was well known for fostering musical talent. Our choirs used to compete at the Feis Cheoil in Dublin and it was rare for us not to win at least one cup.

Being away at school did make me in some ways more self-reliant and, like all girls of my age, I could not wait to get out of school and into the big wide world. I got quite a reasonable Leaving Cert. and the nuns wanted me to go to university, but I told my father that I did not want to consider this. I was hell-bent on doing a course in hotel management but my family was equally determined to prevent me from doing so. In those days such a career was considered to be a very strenuous one for a young lady. The work was regarded as tantamount to slavery and my father certainly did not see a career in hotel management as being suitable for his daughter. I was bitterly disappointed by his obstinacy as I had taken the competitive examination at the School of Catering in Cathal Brugha Street in Dublin and was offered a place on the course. It was not until some years later, when I worked in a college of catering in England, that I could see that my father was right—if for the wrong reasons!

It was decided that I would go to Dublin to do a secretarial course and then take the bank examinations or attempt to get a secretarial post in Guinnesses. Such positions were highly regarded in those days and competition for them was quite fierce. Women like me in Ireland at that time were educated to be wives of middle-class, successful men—and mothers in due course. Any career taken up in the interim period between school and marriage was very much a holding position. It was, therefore, very important that we should choose wisely when it came to husbands and it went without saying that we should keep ourselves for our husbands and not allow our moral character to be tarnished in any way. One can imagine, then, the consternation that would be caused in any family, especially in rural or small-town Ireland, by a daughter who became pregnant outside marriage. A father's hopes would be shattered for ever. A mother, too, would consider that she had failed terribly in her life's work if she did not see her daughter, dressed in white, walk down the aisle on the father's arm. In some cases marriages did go ahead rather hurriedly, but if a girl's delicate condition were known to the clergy, she would then be married in the sacristy and not at the altar-rail—a public, humiliating announcement to the community of her wantonness!

CHAPTER TWO

Like other young women of my generation, I could not wait to be off out into the wide world. The fact that so many of us were incarcerated in convents and boarding schools for our teenage years made the burst for freedom all the more imperative. It wasn't that we wanted to run riot so much as to be able to make our own decisions as regards even the more mundane aspects of life, such as where to live, what to wear and whom to choose as friends.

I worked in secretarial positions in and around Dublin for a few years after leaving St Mary's College, Arklow. I soon made friends with other girls in similar jobs and we eventually graduated from living in hostels to flat-land. Such a life had a magic of its own, certainly initially, as we got our first real taste of freedom. In seemed that after our day's or week's work we had few worries except what to do with our free time. For some of us, the freedom of Dublin during the working week was counterbalanced by being effectively kept in custody in our homes in the country for the weekend. Many of us left the city by bus or train on Friday evening, only returning late on Sunday evening or even early on Monday morning.

During the week there was a great wealth of entertainment available in Dublin. In term-time we had the choice of several university hops, which were then held in the centre of the city. At weekends there were always rugby-club dances in such places as Belvedere or Lansdowne. It was usual for us girls to go to such events in twos or threes: the dances did not end until well after midnight but the last bus ran at eleven-thirty so we often had to walk home. Looking back on it now, it seems we were gluttons for punishment, but at that time we thought nothing of walking several miles home after dancing for three or four hours on end. University students, in the main, did not have cars, unless they were Dubliners who happened to be able to borrow the family car. If any male student did have a car for the evening and offered a girl a lift home, it usually meant that the poor fellow had to bring all the girl's friends home as well!

We often formed relationships with young men we met at these dances and "lines" sometimes went on for several months before couples broke up. The girls were devastated at times but they would meet someone else before long and so the merry-go-round kept twirling. These "lines" did lead to engagements and marriage for some of my friends, who then moved to the next stages of middle-class life: the white wedding, the new home and the new career as wife and home-maker.

I was introduced to John at a hop in Dublin. He was with a group of friends and we were immediately attracted to each other. He was some years older than me and I think that was part of his attraction as he appeared much more sophisticated than most of the other young men we met. We went around for some time as part of a group until he needed a partner for a dress-dance in the Shelbourne Hotel around Christmas time and he asked me if I would like to go with him. I jumped at the chance, as such events were the major events of the social calendar in Dublin and great opportunities to dress up. Our dance was a wonderful evening. During the course of it John told me that he had plans to go to Australia to earn enough money to start up his own business at home. He was planning to leave about three months later and preparations for visa, work permit and so on were well in hand. I was taken aback by the news as I had always imagined that he would in time take over the family business in Ireland. It was in the context of his imminent departure that we went too far and made love about three or four weeks before his departure for Australia in the spring.

His leaving did not in the end cause me too much upset—or at least that is what I told myself. I did not see him off at the airport as I did not want to meet all his family. We said our goodbyes in private at a little party given by one of his friends. That was to be the end of the relationship as far as I was concerned. After all, I was young and, as the saying goes, there were plenty of other fish in the sea.

About four weeks after John's departure I began to feel very unwell, especially in the mornings. My periods had been irregular for many years and for some time I did not give a thought to the possibility that I might be pregnant. I was well into the third month of my pregnancy when one day the penny dropped and I realised that I was in deep trouble. I had been at work that day and rushed home to get ready to go out again. I had a dizzy spell and ended up in a heap on the floor. When I came to, the anxious face of my flatmate was bending over me. Instead of going out as I had planned, I spent the evening alone in my room, trying to come to terms with what was happening. It never occurred to me to go to a doctor at this stage. The longer I could put that off, the greater my chance of denying the truth, especially to myself!

Being pregnant and unmarried in Ireland in the sixties was the most horrific experience imaginable. Words can scarcely express the devastation I experienced. I wished that the world would stop revolving and that somehow I could be hurled off into oblivion, never to be seen or heard of again. Of course, I soon realised that such wishing was pointless and that I would have to come to terms with the fact of pregnancy and the inevitability of motherhood.

Once the initial shock had worn off I began to turn my mind to the practicalities of the situation. I knew that I somehow had to tell my parents what had happened to me. How, in God's name, was I to do it? I knew what desolation it would cause and how long it would take them to come to terms with the shock and the lasting shame. The more I thought about it, the more convinced I became that the longer I could put off the evil day of revelation, the better. I was of very slight build, so with a bit of luck I could continue to work for some months without anyone noticing my condition.

I naturally thought of telling John about this development, but decided against it. He was too far away in Australia and when we parted I saw no future in the relationship. I had no reason now to change my mind.

I took myself up to Gardiner Street to the Jesuit church. I had for some time known a priest there and I desperately needed to talk to someone about my pregnancy and to try and work out what my next move should be. When I arrived at the church in the early evening Father Val was just finishing hearing confessions so I took the opportunity of going to confession. Afterwards, I can remember sitting in the large dimly-lit church waiting for him to emerge from the confessional. I had come to him mainly for spiritual guidance and an opportunity to talk things over and I was surprised when he asked if he could be of any practical help to me. I was grateful for any help I could get, and he found a place for me with a young married couple and family in Dublin. It seemed I could find refuge with them as soon as I felt I needed to. The husband would be out at work all day and the wife was in need of company and perhaps a little help with their young son. It was felt that this would give me a chance to think things through and also to tell my family about my situation when I judged the time to be right.

When I eventually made my journey home to tell my parents at least it was with the knowledge that I had already made my plans and could remove myself quickly from the scene if things became too difficult.

My parents were appalled by my news and, after the initial shock had worn off, frantic to know what to do with me. I made it clear that marriage to John was not an option as far as I was concerned. They decided that I would have to move away from home in order to prevent the neighbours from talking. The baby would naturally have to be given up for adoption. I had little choice but to go along with their decisions and, in fairness to them, I too considered that adoption was the only option at this stage. As for getting away from home, I could hardly wait to do so.

Within a matter of ten days or so I had an appointment with the adoption agency I had chosen to arrange the adoption of my baby when the time came.

The interview with the sister in charge at the adoption agency was everything I had dreaded it would be. I presented myself at the appointed time of four in the afternoon and was left sitting in the waiting room for about fifteen minutes: the previous interview had run over time. I had nothing to do but sit and squirm and imagine all the questions I was going to be asked. I had to tell myself over and over that I was not a *bad* person. But how was I going to convey this to the powers-that-be in the adoption agency?

This was Ireland at a time when sins against the sixth commandment were considered very serious indeed and everything relating to sexual intercourse and pregnancy was regarded as the fault of the woman alone. It had been drummed into us girls from our earliest years that boys were easily led and that it was the responsibility of the girls not to let anything happen. Looking back on this now, it amazes me that we women actually believed this and did not try to reason it out for ourselves. To live through the early years of your womanhood believing, as I did, that women were walking occasions of sin, must have blighted the minds and emotions not only of my generation of young women but of many generations before us.

While I was still mulling over such thoughts I was summoned into the presence of the sister in charge. She was exactly what I had expected. She was, no doubt, imbued with the same ethos as my own, and was determined to make sure that my credentials were up to scratch: that I had come from a good middle-class family; that I had received a good education, at least to secondary level; that I was sound in body and mind and, not least, that the father of my child was not some degenerate. It was also important to satisfy her that I was receiving medical attention to ensure that the baby would be born in good health and with all faculties intact.

I sat in the chair in front of the desk and answered her questions to the best of my ability, hoping that at the end of the interview she would agree to accept me on her agency's register. I had to answer enquiries about the father, where he was, if he was aware of my condition, if not, whether I intended to inform him of it. Some discussion took place regarding the adoption procedure but I can barely recall what was said, other than that I would be parted from my baby at the time of birth, that I would not see the baby at all, that I would be asked to sign preliminary adoption papers after the birth and that the child would be placed with an adoptive family at the age of six weeks. After I left the nursing home where I gave birth, the baby would be sent to Fairy Hill Baby Home to await a placement. For the six-week period until placement, I would pay the baby's maintenance fees in the home.

That appeared to be it, in a nutshell. It was really all very simple, if you could view it with professional detachment and didn't happen to be the natural mother. While the information was being fed to me, I was conscious of being appraised by this no doubt well-meaning woman, and I felt that I was being viewed with a mixture of contempt and pity. I couldn't tell which of these two attitudes I found harder to bear.

After we had discussed the financial aspects and the sister in charge had convinced herself that I knew all that I needed to know, I was free to go. Is it any wonder that I found myself in a complete daze once I was out in the street? I felt as if I was outside myself as I walked back towards O'Connell Street and went into the Monument Creameries to have a cup of coffee. I must have sat there alone for a very long time, trying to piece my thoughts together and forcing myself to realise that I would have to play the game by their rules from now on.

CHAPTER THREE

I was awakened abruptly by the alarm clock on the bedside table. It was six-thirty and still dark in my room. As I turned to silence the clock, I noticed the landing light shining under the bedroom door. That meant only one thing: my mother was already downstairs getting breakfast. I remember thinking how strange things are, that the ordinary patterns of life never seem to change despite terrible upheaval and trauma. Even now I can scarcely imagine how great a shock my disgrace was for my parents, how very hurt and disappointed they must have been. Living as we did in a small town, it was very difficult for them to maintain a façade of normality and calm, all the while trying to come to terms with their own anguish and bewilderment.

I slipped quietly out of bed, trying to move about my room without making too much noise. I did not wish to disturb my father, who was sleeping in the room next door. I had spoken to him the previous evening and I felt that we had said all we needed to say and that there was no point in making it any harder for either of us. I had no intention of marrying the father of my child, even if I could have done so, and my father was wise enough to appreciate that a shotgun marriage was not the solution. What I needed from marriage was a relationship that would endure. I had no desire to face my father again. I could not bear to watch his face, to see the hurt in his eyes. At the time, I could see only disapproval and it was much later that I came to realise how devastated he felt and how worried he must have been about me. My mother, on the other hand, appeared to be made of sterner stuff and, although similarly distraught, coped with things in her own way. For as long as I could remember, way back in my childhood, my mother's way of coping with anything was not to talk about it. It was her way of pretending that something had never happened. She would carry on doing her chores around the house, looking after the family, all the time moving from one practical exercise to another as if her life depended on it. She was a very devoted mother and wife but absolutely hopeless at handling any kind of emotional crisis.

When I finally arrived downstairs for breakfast that morning it was as if nothing significant was taking place in the household. As always, the breakfast table was set in the dining-room, our kitchen of the sixties being rather small. The radio was turned on for the news and I was grateful for the background noise that eased the silence between the two of us. It seemed an age before my brother, Michael, joined us. He was about to return to his teaching job in England and would accompany me on the bus as far as Dublin. He came and sat opposite me at the table and my mother occupied herself in tending to his needs. I was grateful for his presence as it meant that I was no longer the sole focus of her attention. I was happy just to sit there and half-listen to the conversation between them as their voices blended with that of the radio announcer.

In retrospect, I realise that it must have been a doubly distressing morning for my mother, with her son going away to Liverpool for some time and her daughter about to spend several months in Dublin for a very different reason. Both of us would be out of reach and I'm sure that she shed many a tear in private on that morning of our departure.

Once the ritual of breakfast was over, we collected our belongings, my brother carrying the two suitcases downstairs. As we stood on the doorstep in the cold morning air, I turned to bid my mother goodbye, all the time trying to maintain an air of casual normality. I was hurting inside, but I did not wish to distress my mother further by letting her see this. Nothing much was said, but she gave each of us in turn a hug and a kiss before we moved towards the gate and over the dark, deserted street to the square, where we would catch the early-morning bus to Dublin. I didn't look back to see the lonely figure standing in the doorway watching her children leave.

The square was almost deserted, except for the occasional dog running about and rummaging among the dustbins and cardboard boxes of rubbish piled outside the shops for collection. I noticed Bill, the postman, as he delivered the morning post and in the distance I could hear the jingle of milk bottles being delivered by John, the local milkman.

Seeing Bill made me remember what my mother had said to me some days previously. She told me that when I wrote to her I should not put my address on the letters or make any reference to my physical condition, lest the post should go astray. In turn, she would post her letters to me in the postbox at the bottom of the hill and not in the local post-office, in case the ever-vigilant and astute postmistress would notice the address and draw her own conclusions as to my whereabouts and the reason for my prolonged absence. This level of subterfuge seems to me now to be almost farcical, but one must remember that the time in question was the early sixties, when secrets such as mine were kept very dark indeed. Enormous efforts would be made by my family to protect my interests and good name and the respected position they held in the community.

That morning there was the usual assortment of people waiting in a huddle at the bus-stop outside the chemist's in the square. It didn't do to be there too early as the bus was frequently late and the intending passengers had to wait under the elements. This morning was no exception. In my condition the smell of diesel tended to make me nauseous and I really could not afford to be sick so early in the morning. What would the local gossips have done with that piece of news? Normality being the order of the day, I was soon engaged in conversation with two girls who were on their way to Dublin to do an examination for a job in Guinnesses. I had known Jacinta and Mary for some years when we were in primary school. Their father was a local businessman and, like my own father, served on many of the local church and parish committees. The girls were nervous about the examination they were about to take and chatted on incessantly, barely aware of my replies. Michael had met an old rugby friend, and they were busy setting the sporting scene to rights.

In a short time the bus arrived and the passengers lost no time in getting on board. Michael sat beside me and did his best to keep a conversation going, but it was difficult not to be overheard, so for much of the journey we sat in companionable silence. I was just as glad of this because I knew that I would very soon be completely on my own in Dublin and I felt I might as well get used to the situation. I thought of what the next few months might hold. Father Val, my Jesuit friend, who had made the arrangements with the family I was to stay with, had told me that Maria, the wife, was Spanish, that she got a bit lonely during the day while her husband, David, was at work, and would be delighted to have company. I was anxious about meeting them both and wondered whether they would turn out to be just as disapproving of me as everyone else appeared to be. My thoughts began to turn to self-pity, a luxury I couldn't afford, and I had to take myself in hand.

Once the bus reached the centre of Dublin I disembarked at the taxi-rank on the quays and Michael got off the bus with me to put my bags on a taxi. He had little time to bid me goodbye, as the bus was waiting for him to get on again. Kissing me briefly, he said goodbye, asked me to keep in touch and said some encouraging words. Then he was gone.

Getting into the back seat of the car, I asked the taxi-driver to take me to Mespil Road, Ballsbridge. The radio was going full blast and I could barely make myself heard. It was nice not to have to engage in conversation during the twenty-minute journey to the house that was to be my home until my baby was born.

While I was living with my host family of David and Maria, I had plenty of time to ruminate on my life. Although I spent quite a lot of the day keeping Maria company and helping her about the place, time hung heavy on my hands when, for instance, she took the baby, Stephen, for a walk. I would then find myself face to face with the reality: I was twenty, single, pregnant and in hiding in Dublin, even going so far as to use the pseudonym Mary O'Dwyer in all my dealings with people.

I was living in the nice residential area of Ballsbridge, which was then at a remove from the city centre. The apartment, though small, was quite adequate. I made the usual visits to my obstetrician. He was to me a compassionate and understanding man, not in the least condemnatory; perhaps he felt he could leave that to others who deemed themselves better qualified. I remember on one occasion being in his rooms when he received an emergency call and had to rush away to attend to another patient of his, a young woman who had slit her wrists. At the time it seemed to me to be either a desperate attempt to end it all or else a plea for understanding of her predicament. I could well identify with her emotions and knew how alone she must feel. I also realised that there were others worse off than myself.

My parents had warned me not to go out too often in daylight in the city for fear that someone from home would see me, so I often went out for a walk alone after dark. The streets were usually very quiet then, with perhaps a few people walking around like myself. Every so often a bus would come rushing past, usually full of chatting passengers, who were visible in the well-lit interior. I would feel very much alone as I watched the buses disappear from view and I would imagine to myself these same passengers returning home to waiting family and friends. To distract myself, I would look up into the night sky and watch the flickering stars and the moon hiding itself behind the clouds and re-emerging. My mind would drift back to my home and to other parts of Ireland I knew well. Having exhausted myself with walking, I would return to the apartment with a prayer that I would sleep well that night. Sometimes my prayer was answered but there were many nights when an overactive mind kept me awake plotting and planning all the wonderful things I would do as soon as I became part of the human race again.

During the day, in order that I might escape into the open from time to time, I decided that it was necessary to adopt some form of camouflage. I bought a pair of very dark navy-blue-rimmed sunglasses, which I now feel quite sure did little to disguise my identity, given that the months of September, October and November in Ireland are not noted for bright sunshine. What a peculiar sight I must have been! I was fortunate, however, that a relative of my host took me some evenings to an out-of-town pub or restaurant. Going into the city to a cinema was out of the question, as cinemas were frequented by university students and I might be spotted. There was, interestingly enough, no restriction on attending Sunday Mass; perhaps it was felt that the Lord would make me invisible or that the congregation would be so elevated by prayer that nobody would notice me.

My home might well have been on the other side of the world, so far out of my reach was it until such time as I was in a position to return. I often wondered how my parents were coping. I imagined them as they went on with their lives, maintaining a semblance of normality but feeling terrible hurt and worried inside. I was sure that they often wondered where they had gone wrong with me.

My mother wrote to me every week. The letters were full of routine happenings, news of my father and of Michael. She said very little about how anyone was feeling. My father would drive my mother to Dublin to see me about once every four weeks, but he never came in to see me himself. I suppose I thought at the time that he was too embarrassed to do so, preferring to leave that side of things to my mother as she did so much of what was considered "women's work." She would arrive with a home-made cake for me, often a chocolate sandwich, which she knew I liked very much. We would sit together making stilted conversation, both careful not to reveal anything of our true feelings. If I had been honest I would have admitted how much I hated these visits and wished that my parents would not come to Dublin at all. I always felt so uncomfortable and guilt-ridden when they left. I just wished that everyone who knew me would let me alone to cope as best I could. It was so much easier to retain a stiff upper lip when loved ones were out of sight and out of mind. Many a night I cried myself to sleep out of sheer frustration.

CHAPTER FOUR

The taxi was late. It had been booked well in advance by my hosts, Maria and David, as they knew that I had to be at the nursing home by ten that morning. I was in a state of near-panic as I heaved my now distended body on to the window-seat on the landing above the hall door. I could get a good view of the road from there. I had no sooner settled myself comfortably than I saw the car arrive. The driver looked somewhat harassed and, opening his side window to get a better view of the house number, he beeped the horn. This sudden noise was the signal for pandemonium to break loose! The family dogs began to bark loudly as they were wont to do when strangers arrived. Stephen, no doubt woken by the barking, began to scream his head off.

David was by this time ushering me and Maria, who was to accompany me, down the front steps and into the taxi. Placing my small suitcase on the back seat of the car, he turned to me and enclosed me in a bear-hug, saying, "Goodbye, Mary, take good care of yourself. We will be waiting for the news. Don't worry about a thing."

Maria was anxious to get going straight away and she pushed David aside, reminding him that we were already late and urging him to look after Stephen. As the taxi sped down the road, she again gave the driver the address of our destination, reminding him that we were thirty minutes late. He apologised, mentioning heavy traffic on the north side of the city on the way to the airport.

I felt very apprehensive about what I was heading into, having left the familiar surroundings of what had become home to me over the previous three months. Maria and David had been very kind and she and I had become good friends. They were not that much older than me and I felt less ill at ease in their company than I would have done with older people. They could not deny or ignore the fact that I was pregnant and unmarried, but somehow they were able to look beyond that and accept me for the person I really was. We had enjoyed ourselves together and I was able to participate in the fun of family life. At other times, however, I could not help feeling lonely, abandoned and bewildered and I had to make great efforts to convince myself that I would eventually emerge from this nightmare and that the future would have something brighter to offer me.

I was lost in thought as the car moved out towards Ranelagh, barely conscious of the voices of Maria and the taxi-driver as they chatted. As we drew near to the nursing home, which I had seen previously on one occasion, my heart began to race and the palms of my hands were soaked with perspiration. I was very frightened, wondering how I would be able to cope. I was not yet in labour, as I was going to be induced, but it would have perhaps been better if I had been in some sort of physical discomfort. I knew that I would be in pain before long but had no way of imagining how severe it would be, how long it would last, whether I would be left alone to get on with it. Would I be given something to ease the pain or would I be made to suffer for my wrongdoing? My mind was in turmoil. I had only a vague notion of what the natural course of events would be and I was also very conscious that once Maria had settled me in, she would need to return to her own home immediately to look after Stephen and let David get to work.

The taxi turned in at the driveway of St Imelda's Nursing Home. Maria was out of the car in a flash and as she paid the driver, she said to me, "Here we are at last, Mary. We'd better get inside." Seeing my crestfallen expression, she added that she would make the excuses for our delay to Matron. The hall door was opened by the Matron herself, a tall slender woman in her fifties. She shook hands with us to welcome us and led the way upstairs to the top of the house and a small bedroom to the rear. "Now, Miss O'Dwyer," she said to me, "you can unpack. Your friend will help you. Then get undressed and into bed and I'll be back to see you in about half an hour. There's another lady about to deliver at any moment and I must see to her."

After she left, I sat on the bed and cried. Maria came over and hugged me. "Ah, Mary, why is it that we women are always given the most awful jobs?" She did her best to console me and then started putting my room to rights. Still sitting on the bed, I began to undress. As I pulled my maternity dress over my head for the last time, I held it out in front of me as if to say goodbye to it. In a strange sort of way, it seemed that by casting the garment from me I was passing a milestone in my life. I remember shivering slightly as I crumpled the dress in my hands and threw it on the floor. Maria, watching me out of the corner of her eye as she busied herself about the room, said nothing but stooped down and picked up the dress. She put it into a carrier bag she had brought with her. "Mary, you won't need this any more so I'll take it back with me." I could only smile weakly at her through my tears.

I struggled into my white gown and tumbled into bed, settling the starched bedclothes around me. Then it was time for Maria to leave, after hugging me goodbye and reassuring me that I could get in touch with her or David by telephone if I needed anything. I sat up in bed and listened to the sound of silence. I was certainly on my own now.

The remainder of that day can only be described as a nightmare. Soon after Maria left I was prepared for the process of giving birth. I felt such a sense of detachment that it was as if I was some kind of spectator of the events going on before my eyes, while all the time knowing that *I* was the person who was centre-stage. After being given an injection to induce labour, I was tucked up in bed and left alone for over an hour while the drug took effect. Occasionally Matron or her assistant came in to cast an eye on me, but there was no question of anyone offering me company or comfort. Eventually the pain grew more intense, my waters broke and it was established that I was well on my way. As Matron and her assistant stood on either side of my bed, I was conscious of a conversation taking place from which I was totally excluded. I can only suppose that I retreated into my own little world, holding on to whatever shreds of dignity remained to me by telling myself that it could not be too long before I was through with all this. The pain intensified but it was some time before I was ready to deliver. During this time, I drifted in and out of a stupor, conscious of strangers in the room with me all the time. I vaguely heard mention of a telephone call being made to my obstetrician to inform him that it was nearly time to attend me and I remember coming out of my stupor sufficiently to recognise his face as he came in the bedroom door.

After this, I was gently eased towards the edge of the bed, ether was administered to me and I was knocked out cold. I cannot say that I was really frightened but I *was* totally humiliated. There was no humanity at all in the procedure; I might as well have been a farrowing sow. I expect I was just another patient as far as my medical attendants were concerned, but the indignity of it all is stamped on my memory forever.

I awoke from my drug-induced sleep at about 7.20 that evening. I was informed that the baby was a girl and that she was quite small but otherwise fit and well. I was given a light supper and allowed to see Maria for a few minutes. I asked Maria to go and see the baby as I knew I would not be allowed to do so, and I dearly wanted to know what she looked like. (It was regarded at the time as the best course of action for the pregnant girl to be anaesthetised at the end of labour and thereafter to be prevented from seeing her baby at all, in the case of the baby being given up for adoption.) Was she pretty? What colour were her eyes and hair? Maria did not have time that evening to see the baby, but on a subsequent visit she did manage to get to see her. Having one's baby described by a third party is a very poor substitute for being able to see her oneself. Maria reported that she was indeed tiny, that she had lots of black hair, very small eyes and a very red face. That was the picture of my daughter that I was to carry in my mind's eye for the rest of my life! I never thought of asking for someone to take a photograph but I'm sure it would have been out of the question.

I cannot begin to describe how I felt as I was put to bed that evening after giving birth to my baby. During the night I awoke occasionally and automatically my hand would go to my stomach to check that the bump had gone. In one way it was a relief to reassure myself, but also a great sadness to think that part of me was gone forever and that I would never again see my child this side of eternity. I knew she was downstairs in the nursery, only a short distance away, but it might as well have been thousands of miles, for if I had gone downstairs and taken a look at her I would have broken the rules of the adoption agency and they could have refused to place her for adoption. My only option seemed to be to play the game by the agency's rules.

The days passed somehow and I gradually got stronger. In the main, the radio was my only company, apart from visits from Maria and a few very close friends. There would be no joyous announcement of the birth in the social and personal columns of the newspapers.

One of the chaplains to the adoption agency, a shy,

retiring man who did little to put me at my ease, called to see me one afternoon to arrange for the baby's christening. I already knew the name—Claire—that I would give my daughter, although her adopters would have every right to call her something else entirely.

Before I left the nursing home, Matron reassured me that I had done the right thing in choosing to give up my baby for adoption and that now it was best for me to forget her entirely. I should put all this behind me and go out and make a new life for myself and in time I should be grateful that I had made the right decision. My baby would be placed with a good family that could provide her with all the things I would be unable to provide. Someone, it appeared, would be happy as a result of all of this—but I knew for sure it would not be me.

I packed my few personal belongings and stood in the chill of the little bedroom I had occupied for ten days, and again I felt a huge sense of aloneness. My heart was heavy as I made my way down the long winding stairs to the main hall. There I said goodbye to Matron and walked out to join Maria in a taxi. "Don't look back, Mary," Matron had said to me. I heard the click of the door as it closed behind me and instead of looking back I quickened my step until I was safely inside the taxi. Then Maria's arm was around my shoulders and as the taxi joined the traffic on the road outside, I saw the lights of the city shining through my tears.

CHAPTER FIVE

After spending a few days with Maria and David, I was to return once again to the bosom of my own family. I was not looking forward to this. I wanted, above all, to get away from everybody and everything that had been close to me. The last thing I needed was incarceration at home for weeks on end with my mother fussing over my physical welfare, making sure I got enough rest, that I had the right kind of food, and ensuring, once I was strong enough, that I got out for a long walk each day in the clean, fresh air of the countryside. I was now, however, at my parents' mercy: I had no job and had exhausted my savings so I had little option but to submit to a period of small-town life until I could get into the swing of things again. At the time it seemed to me that I had little say in anything and that it was easier to swim with the tide than to risk ending up on the rocks.

My father had his work to go to each day, so there would be some escape from his disapproving glance, at least until the late afternoon. My sudden reappearance in our small-town society would be explained by my parents leading everyone to believe that I had been a little under the weather, as a consequence of not looking after myself properly in that flat in Dublin. Life would be very simple again, if we didn't allow ourselves to be confused.

My parents called to Mespil Road for me in the early evening. My mother came into the house for a few minutes to meet the family before collecting my suitcase. My father remained in the car. It was obvious that he did not want to make a big thing of my coming home or to get involved with my friends. I was quite saddened by this as I felt close to Maria and David and grateful to them for all that they had done. My father was not normally a rude man, in fact quite the opposite, and so I can only imagine that he felt so embarrassed about everything that he preferred to keep his distance and hope that this would make the whole incident easier to forget. There was nothing unusual in this for a reticent man of his generation.

The journey home was quite tense. My father drove while I sat in silence beside my mother in the back. The evening was drawing in and I was grateful for the darkness as I felt less self-conscious and knew that I could at least think my thoughts in peace without their showing on my face. I was going to have plenty of time to dwell on certain aspects of my life so I might as well get used to introspection. I couldn't really think of anything to say to my parents and any attempt on my part to make light conversation would have sounded hollow and would in the end have reduced me to tears. So I just sat and thought and tried to keep my dignity by focusing on the things I would be able to do once I escaped to freedom again.

As we neared home, my father said to me, "Now that you are home again, we must put the past behind us. Your mother and I are deeply saddened by what happened. We do not intend to say anything more about it. You must concentrate on getting well and getting on with your life." Would that it were to be so simple!

Supper was rather strange. My mother had made my favourite cake, a chocolate sandwich, and as I looked from it to my parents' sombre faces I came to the conclusion that, while in their hearts they might have been happy to have me home again, they were completely unable to convey that feeling to the person who mattered most—me.

As I went up to bed that night, I could not decide whether I was glad or sorry to be home. I was back in my own bedroom, with all my familiar things around me. When I turned off my bedside lamp I could see, once again, the landing light shining under the bedroom door, and I recalled how much had happened since the morning of my departure for Dublin. I could hear the familiar sounds coming from downstairs: the radio in the background and the muffled sounds of my parents' voices. I tried to imagine what they were talking about.

I knew that I would have to face the neighbours and townspeople sooner or later. In the main they were kindly people doing their best to live their lives and rear their families. I often wonder how many other local families went through the same trauma and lived in fear of the local gossips. Soon after midnight the streetlights went out and as I waited for sleep to come I resolved that the next day I would begin to rebuild my future from the ashes of the past.

The following week passed uneventfully. I was more or less confined to base and watched the outside world from behind the curtains of our front windows: the people going about their daily business; the children on their way to and from school; the faithful going to Mass on Sunday. I wished I could be among them instead of hiding until it was considered fitting by my family for me to rejoin the human race.

The guilt and embarrassment I felt are difficult to convey, or even to recall for myself. I had committed the cardinal sin, almost the only sin as far as Catholic Ireland was concerned. If the news ever broke in my hometown I would be ruined for ever. It is a frightful burden to place on any young girl's shoulders: to make her feel so wicked about something that in another context would be regarded as a blessing and a cause for celebration. The fact that I did not have a ring on my finger made the difference between my being regarded as good or evil. Is it any wonder that some girls in my position were so distraught as to take their own lives or run away to England to escape? Nobody seemed to care a jot about the wounded and vulnerable young mother who would be haunted for the rest of her life by the loss of her baby. Was that not punishment enough for any woman?

It was perhaps a mercy that at this time I accepted so readily what the people in the agency had told me—that it was feasible for me to build a new life and put the past behind me. I am sure that this is what I wanted to believe. I now realise, however, that it was not possible. The years ahead were certainly difficult for me. Birthdays, Christmas and other family celebrations were painful hurdles. At such times, amidst the laughter and togetherness, I could not but remember the little one who was missing. It was harder for me to bear because the anguish had to be hidden behind a façade of normality and good spirits. In time, I became such a mistress of the masquerade that I managed to convince even myself that all was well.

CHAPTER SIX

It was almost eight months after the birth of Claire. The awful day dawned at last, the day I had been dreading for weeks. On this day it would be necessary for me to return to the adoption agency in order to sign the final papers that would separate me from my daughter for ever.

My father was to drive me to Dublin. He would then leave me in the afternoon and I would go to the agency alone. As far as I can remember, he had business with an educational publisher regarding the selection of schoolbooks for the next school year. I remembered wistfully how, in previous years, when I was still living at home, I had looked forward to such trips to Dublin with him. They were an annual highlight. We would buy the books for his school and then, after lunch at Bewleys or Clerys we would go shopping for something for me to wear. We seemed to be very close in those days; now we were like strangers. Only now that I look back from the vantage point of years can I see just how hurt and heartbroken he must have been. His coldness and remoteness arose not so much from disapproval as from helplessness, and were probably the only way he had of dealing with his pain. I expect he felt that if he had shown sympathy towards me at any stage, my resolve might have weakened, and there would have been floods of tears and a refusal on my part to comply with whatever would be demanded of me by the adoption agency.

We ate a silent lunch together in Bewleys, every mouthful of food painful for me to swallow. I left my father outside the GPO and made my way to Henry Street. I felt utterly alone, as if everyone belonging to me was dead. When I reached the door of the agency, I looked around to make sure that there was nobody about who might recognise me. I pushed open the heavy black-painted door with its polished brass knocker and discreet brass name-plate, and made my way along the semi-dark and airless hall and up the highly polished linoleum-covered stairway to the large musty room which served as a reception area for callers. There was a partition of timber and frosted glass in which there was a service hatch with a bell for callers to ring for attention. As I rang the bell I could hear female voices engaged in conversation at the other side of the hatch and then it was opened by a woman of mature years. After I had haltingly announced my business, I was asked to take a seat and told that Sister would be informed of my arrival.

I sat at the table in a Victorian spoon-backed chair and I took note of everything around me. There was an air of frugality about the place. The paintwork was a dull, dirty cream and the wallpaper was faded with wear in places and in other places water-stained. I was conscious of an atmosphere of helplessness and despair and felt that there ought to have been a poster at the reception area captioned, "Abandon hope, all ye who enter here." There were magazines on the table but I was in no fit state of mind to read them. As far as I can recall, they were mainly out-of-date copies of *The Messenger of The Sacred Heart*, *The Far East* and other such religious publications.

I sat alone in the reception room until about fifteen minutes after the time scheduled for my appointment. Then a woman in her mid-thirties emerged from the door beside the glass partition. She was beautifully dressed in a restrained sort of way, in a tweed suit and pearls with matching shoes and handbag. A nun with a beaming smile was ushering her out, a nun I recognised from my previous visit as the sister in charge. Once the woman had left and her footsteps had faded down the stairs, the sister turned to me and said, "Come along, Mary, and let us see what is to be done." I rose from my chair and followed her into her office like a lamb to the slaughter.

Her office was really no improvement on the ante-room in which I had been waiting. Settling herself behind the large, heavily carved mahogany desk on which lay neatly arranged files and piles of paper, Sister Eucharia rested her elbows on the edge of the desk. She pushed back the wide sleeves of her habit and selected the appropriate file from among the bundles in front of her. She perused the contents for a few seconds before saying, "Now, let me see. Yes, it is now six months since your baby was placed with a family, so it will be necessary for you to go today to sign the final papers. There is not much to it, really. I have arranged an appointment for you with our solicitors.

Now go along, Mary, down to Mr Duffy. His office is only a few doors away from here and he will look after the necessary legal matters. You will have to swear on the Bible as to your identity and your signature but he will guide you through it all, so there is really nothing to worry about. After you have finished with Mr Duffy, come back here to me."

I left the office without saying anything. As I went down the stairs, I held tightly to the banisters for fear of losing my footing on the highly polished linoleum. It would never do for me to fall, as I felt that the slightest upset would shatter my fragile façade of composure. It was as if my inner self was already dying and I was mourning it without any outward display of grief. I told myself over and over again that I was doing the right thing—the only possible thing—and that I had somehow better pull myself together. After all, I had to display a certain degree of normality; otherwise those in authority might well decide that I was mentally unbalanced and suspect that my child had inherited similar characteristics. This fear was not totally without foundation as I remembered being told at one of my interviews with the adoption agency that the mother had to be of sound moral character and that the child would need to be both physically and mentally sound.

I found the solicitor's office without any difficulty. On the doorstep I hesitated for a few seconds in an effort to calm myself and sort out my thoughts. I noticed immediately that the lawyer's office and the adoption agency were both tatty and run-down; perhaps they were even owned by the same uncaring landlord. It may appear strange that I was so concerned by the appearance of the buildings but I have always been very sensitive to my surroundings. I was probably concentrating on my surroundings in order to still my deeper feelings of panic and anguish.

Again I had to go upstairs to a reception area. For the second time that day I stated my business, but this time had to wait for only a few minutes. I did consider making at attempt to flee before it was too late, but I came quickly to my senses when I realised the consequences of such a course of action. If I backed away at this stage it was quite possible that I would not be offered a second chance to have my baby adopted. How was I to know how my adopters would react? What kind of people were they anyway? Did they really love my daughter and if I withdrew at this stage would they be broken-hearted? I did not suspect that if I refused to sign the final papers, I would have a lengthy legal struggle to regain my own flesh and blood, even at that stage in the proceedings. I had been given to understand in earlier discussions with the agency that my baby was mine until the final papers were signed. Nobody pointed out that in the event of my changing my mind, the legal expenses I would incur would be way beyond the resources of any young girl without the support of her family. With hindsight, I can see that the legal implications of the whole adoption procedure were very poorly explained to me.

A hand on my arm brought me back from my thoughts to reality as a male voice, that of the solicitor, Mr Duffy, said, "Miss O'Dwyer, I believe you have come to see me. Will you please come this way?" I followed a tallish man of average build in his fifties out of the reception room. He had a rather sterile manner and at times appeared embarrassed, as if he would really have preferred not to be dealing with people like myself—he may have felt very sorry for me or had daughters of his own, but he had to do his job.

In his office the relevant papers were already spread out on his desk. He handed me a small well-worn Bible on which to swear my identity and signature. As he led me through the formalities, I was conscious both of repeating the words after him and at the same time of relinquishing all legal rights to my baby. It was all over in a few seconds: so much disposed of in so little time. As far as I can remember, nothing was said about the irrevocability of what I was doing. Before the ink was dry on the paper, I was on my way back to the adoption agency.

I hated going back there, I was very tired by now and the last thing I wanted was another meeting with Sister Eucharia. I did not need anyone to tell me that I had done the right and sensible thing. I did not need to be told that I had my whole life in front of me, that I was now free to build a new life for myself—that in time, if I was lucky and if it was God's will, I would meet a nice man, who, despite all this, would offer me marriage, a home, and children of my own.

In the event, as I sat opposite Sister Eucharia, I had to listen to most of these platitudes and was made to feel, once again, that really I was getting out of this whole affair very lightly indeed. Despite the smile on the sister's face and her semblance of concern, I sensed a cold air of disapproval. Now I knew a little of what a sinner might feel as she was about to be stoned to death in Biblical times! Finally, just before I left, Sister Eucharia told me that my daughter would be given every chance in life. She was being adopted by a medical family and I was, it seemed, to be grateful for that. As I walked out the door for what I thought would be the last time and joined the crowd in the street, I realised that I was meant to forget completely about my baby daughter.

CHAPTER SEVEN

In the mid-sixties my family decided to move to live in
Kent, in south-east England. My brother, Michael, had
been living and teaching there for some years. He had
recently married and set up home in Ramsgate. My
father, having taught in Ireland for long enough to
qualify for a full pension, decided that the time was now
right for him to experience what teaching in England
would be like. Teachers were in great demand so he had
no difficulty in getting a position in a Catholic school in
Broadstairs. I suspected that he wanted a change for me
also, a chance for me to start afresh, although when I
came to know my father very well at the end of his life,
he never implied that I had anything to do with his
decision to move away from Ireland. In any case, it was
not his intention to end his days in Kent and he maintained
a home in Ireland all the time he was away.

So it was that, still in my early twenties, I left Ireland
with my family to live in Broadstairs, a very pleasant
small coastal town, famous for its connections with
Charles Dickens. I took to life there straight away. As far

as getting a job was concerned, I was spoiled for choice. I took a local government post with the education committee and worked on the administrative staff of a large technical college, near enough to home to enable me to travel to and from work each day.

Before long we became assimilated into the local Catholic community. My father was asked to join the Knights of St Columbanus and his involvement greatly enhanced our social life. There was no shortage of social evenings, dress-dances and other functions where it was possible for me to meet likely young men.

I had been working at the technical college for about a year when I met Michael Batts. He was teaching at the local boys' grammar school and some of the staff used the restaurant which was attached to the catering department of my college. I had seen Michael come and go, then one day he presented himself at the office to ask if he could borrow a long-armed stapler. He had been recruited to edit the school magazine and his own English department did not possess such an item. I can clearly recall making him sign for the stapler and gaining his assurances that it would be returned within the prescribed time. He did return it, along with a copy of the school magazine. Soon an invitation to the Marlowe Theatre followed, and things just went on from there.

We were married in the local Catholic church about a year after we had first met. It was a June wedding and rather a glittering occasion. After a short honeymoon in Sussex, we settled down to married life in a semi-detached house only a short distance away from both our families. I was fortunate in having two sets of good neighbours—both wives were Irish girls.

Our son, Rory, was born the following March. His birth was not particularly easy—he was a big baby of nine pounds—and indeed it was thought at one stage that he would not survive. I am sure now that the problems associated with his birth were not exclusively physical, but psychological as well, a result of Claire's birth and subsequent adoption.

Michael, Rory and I came back to live in Waterford in the early seventies, when Michael took a job in the Regional Technical College there. We remained for ten years, during which time Rory went to primary school and I began to work again on a part-time basis as a substitute teacher, work I greatly enjoyed. When Rory got a bit older, I got a job as an executive secretary/personal assistant to the senior partner in a firm of solicitors. This was my introduction to working with the law and I was hooked from the outset. It was at the time that capital taxation was introduced to replace the old estate duty. I became quite skilled in taxation matters and I was soon given my own portfolio of clients under the supervision of the senior partner. I later became a member of the Institute of Taxation of Ireland.

Eventually Michael was offered a post as head of department in a secondary school in south-east Kent, an opportunity he was keen to take up, and we have lived in this area ever since. When we moved back to England I continued to work in the law. I got a job with a large legal firm in Canterbury and soon became a solicitor's clerk, dealing mainly with criminal litigation, civil litigation and also with some family law. I was in my element and soon found that I could relate very well to clients who were in difficulties.

It seemed, as I approached middle-age, that I had everything I needed for a well-structured and contented lifestyle. I had had nearly twenty-five years of happily married life and I accepted that my times of loneliness and bleakness were no different from what everyone experiences from time to time. The loss of Claire had always been with me and I thought that I had really come to terms with it and could do nothing to change the past.

PART TWO

CHAPTER EIGHT

December 1986

My decision to embark on a search for my daughter came as a surprise, even to me. I had, of course, never forgotten her—what mother could?—but even to contemplate the possibility of finding her seemed totally unrealistic. Twenty-five years had passed since she was handed over to her adoptive parents—a lot of water under the bridge.

In the late autumn of 1986 I embarked on a course of psychotherapy. Over the previous few years I had felt the need to examine my past in some depth as I had from time to time experienced intense restlessness and mild anxiety. It was my GP who initially suggested that I might benefit from psychotherapy. I was willing to give it a try, although it was with feelings of great trepidation that I attended my first session. I discovered that the process was not easy, and that it was not intended for the faint-hearted. It made great demands on my inner strength and would at times be excruciatingly painful. I would have to face myself directly, not knowing what would emerge from the mists of my past.

My first impression of my therapist was of someone aloof and uncommunicative, devoid of feeling, poker-faced and taciturn, a bit like a blank canvas on which, in time, I was going to paint a picture of my life—in blood, sweat and tears if necessary! There were many times I asked myself just what I thought I was doing coming along each week for a fifty-minute session of sheer hell. Was I mad after all? Nevertheless, I was drawn to these sessions as if by some magnetic force. I did eventually begin to open up memories of my childhood and teenage life and onwards, moving into events and experiences of my early womanhood and right through to the present time. Once I had begun to talk about my daughter and the circumstances of her conception, my pregnancy and her birth, it became clear to me that this was at the core of my problems. I realised at this stage where my feelings of restlessness and anxiety had come from. It was as if a great light had been quenched inside me at the time of my separation from my baby, a light that would never be rekindled. It was to take many sessions before I could really accept what had happened to me many years previously and to see that my life had become brittle and fragmented from that time onwards.

It was at a session in early December 1986 that it suddenly became clear to me that I needed to tackle these issues head-on. By the time that session was over I knew that the following options were open to me: I could leave things as they were; I could retreat into the past and allow it to submerge me for ever; I could bite the bullet and move forward by initiating a search for Claire. I decided on the last course.

In March 1987 my mother died unexpectedly. (My father had died ten years before). After the funeral, once the initial shock had worn off, I began to feel a sense of freedom as if, somehow, the time was now right to begin my search for Claire. I do not quite understand why this should be so, but it was as if, in a curious way, I had been given permission to uncover the past.

How and where to begin my search after such a very long time was the next big question. Memories of the period of Claire's birth had been deeply buried as if in a cast-iron vault, never again to be opened. I was, of course, longing to know what had happened to my daughter. There were so many questions to be asked and answered that even to begin to think about her was enough to send me into a trance. I felt that it was only when all these questions had been answered to my satisfaction that I could allow myself the peace that would come with knowing that I had done the right thing by letting her go. So I had to get on with the business of finding her.

Before our marriage, I had told Michael about my past and as I appeared to be content to leave it at that, he did not wish to intrude, even at times when he sensed I was vulnerable and low. For instance, Claire's birthday and Christmases were nightmares for me, as I wondered where Claire was, imagining what she must look like at various stages of her development and, above all, wondered whether she was happy. On such nights, when the house was quiet and my husband and son safely slumbering, I often put my head under the bedclothes and cried myself to sleep, at the same time praying silently for the child I had lost.

In April 1987 I began to make plans for my search. I decided to begin by writing to the adoption agency. I had to find out whether the agency still existed and if so, where it was located. As I was living in England it was not easy to get hold of an Irish telephone directory, but I found one in the local library that was about four years out of date. I could only vaguely remember the name of the agency and was a bit surprised that in no time at all I had its telephone number and address. I decided to write a letter. Having worked for many years as a solicitor's managing clerk, I had some idea how I should approach it. My letter was short and to the point: I was making enquiries about a baby who had been adopted back in 1965 and wondered whether they could help me.

In ten days or so a reply landed on the mat, telling me that the staff of the agency had searched the files and located the relevant papers. They were, however, very sorry to inform me that nothing could be done other than put my letter on file in case my daughter made contact with them at a later date. There had not been any enquiries from her over the years. They advised me that I should keep them up to date with any future change of address. I was bitterly disappointed as it was clear to me that any move for us to make contact must begin with Claire. But at least I was now sure that I had begun to look in the right place. The fact that they could not help me was painful but understandable and I still had plenty of determination to prosecute the search.

In May of 1987 I wrote to Mrs Mary Robinson, barrister-at-law in Dublin, now President of Ireland. She had been a senator for many years and was a well-known champion of women's causes. I thought I would lose nothing by seeking her advice. I was not disappointed: she responded promptly to say that my search "may be possible but could be very difficult." She suggested that I get in touch with a solicitor, an established authority on family law in Ireland, who would be willing to see me to discuss matters at least.

I did as she suggested and this solicitor replied that he would help me if he could. It was, however, late August 1987 before I could travel to Ireland for a holiday and arrange to see him. I outlined my story; he in turn sketched the legal position and pointed out the many difficulties. He told me what my rights and entitlements were—they were very few! I learned from him that birth certificates are public documents and that I was therefore entitled to take up as many as I wished. He also mentioned a government publication dating from the time of Claire's adoption which might give me some information; the problem was that, such material being twenty-three years old, it would be very difficult to get hold of. Even if I acquired it, it could take a very long time indeed to sift through such material without any guarantee of finding what I was looking for—to mention nothing of the expenses I would incur. He did say that for me to avail of the services of his practice would cost me a very great deal, but that if I was minded to undertake the extensive groundwork myself, it might be worth a try. I was left under no illusion: the chances of success were so small that it was like looking for the proverbial needle in a haystack.

When I left the solicitor's office I still felt that it was

worth a try, even though I considered myself to be either mad or desperate—or both! After I had returned home, I was more convinced than ever that I wanted to pursue this search to the end. I think I latched on to Mrs Mary Robinson's phrase "It may be possible." If that were the case, I would pursue it.

CHAPTER NINE

I had often felt that I could be a good investigative journalist and now, it seemed, I had my chance to prove my theory. I also knew that Irish people still made time to help others, and were by nature cordial. I decided to write to the Government Stationery Office in Dublin to ask for back-issues of an Irish newspaper (similar to *The Gazette* in the UK), some twenty-five years old. I soon had a reply that the office did not hold old issues of this publication but they suggested that I try the National Library in Kildare Street in Dublin, where such material was kept on file.

I telephoned the National Library on a dark and dismal afternoon in late September 1987. I felt that I would get further by using a personal approach, especially as I was telephoning from England. I told the young woman who answered my call that I was looking for old copies of the *Uiris Oifigiúil*, from way back in the sixties. She replied that the person who could help me was on his lunch-break but would be back at three o'clock. His name, she said, was Mr Malone.

Later that afternoon, I spoke to the kindly and helpful Mr Malone. Yes, he said, it was certainly possible to get hold of the information I needed. It was no longer kept in hard copy but could be taken from the microfilm records. What exactly did I need? With tongue in cheek and fingers crossed, I breezily replied that I needed details of adoptions in Ireland for the period in question for some research that I had undertaken. He explained that I would need to write to him, stating my requirements precisely. Someone would then Xerox the relevant pages for me at the cost of twenty pence a sheet.

I thanked him for his assistance and said that I would be in touch. I immediately sent off a letter detailing my requirements. I had decided for a start to order copies of the *Uiris* for the last two quarters of 1965, as I imagined that my daughter would have been adopted and the final papers processed by that time. After about three weeks a large brown envelope arrived, so fat that the postman could not push it through the letter-box. My little terriers, Fritz and Bunter, alerted me to the fact that someone was at the door and after the postman had handed me the envelope I pushed the remains of the family breakfast to one side, poured myself a cup of lukewarm tea and opened the package, which was thoroughly sealed with Sellotape. The contents spilled out on the table and I was absolutely amazed by the number of pages of names and addresses of adopters that appeared before my eyes, especially because at the time of my own dealings with the adoption agency I was given to understand that girls like myself were very few and far between. Here in front of my eyes was evidence to the contrary: for the last two quarters of 1965 there were names of at least five hundred adoptions that had been finalised. When I received the list for the first half of 1966, I saw that the total number was almost a thousand.

I stared and stared at these lists and suddenly felt a deep sense of anger and outrage. How dared the adoption agency castigate me all those years before and lead me to believe that I was a terrible deviant for engaging in sexual intercourse outside marriage. The wages of my sin were pregnancy (presumably the direct result of the wrath of God); my punishment the loss of my child for ever by a process known as adoption. There was little compassion for the mother, and the sooner she knew this the better for her.

Even in my anger, however, I saw some humour in the situation. How difficult it must have been to hide away *one thousand* single pregnant woman in 1964/1965. There we were, lurking around corners, ducking and diving, perhaps even trying to avoid one another. Someone made money out of all of this! We had to be accommodated and we had to have medical attention. Hospitals, nursing homes and obstetricians had to be found for us. Some of the smaller, more secret nursing homes must have augmented their income considerably by taking in fallen women, waifs and strays like me. At least I had some say in the matter of the nursing home where I was delivered and the obstetrician who attended me; other unfortunates had no choice but to go to "mother and baby" homes run by nuns especially for single girls. There they sometimes had to work their passage by doing domestic chores. After the birth they had to care for their babies for the six weeks until it was time to give them up to adopters. What heartbreak!—although who could say it was any better to be completely denied any sight of your baby, as I was?

On the morning I received the Xeroxes from the National Library in Dublin, I spent several hours looking at the pages of Christian names of the adopted children, together with the names and addresses of the adoptive families. The solicitor I saw in Dublin had explained to me that the names I had given my daughter when she was christened would almost certainly have been changed by the adopters, so there would be no point in expecting to get a lead from the names. It was, therefore, a form of mental torture for me to gaze on the information on the table in front of me, realising that the answer to all my prayers might be contained there but that I had no way of deciphering it. In an extraordinary sort of way I felt that these papers were in themselves special because of that. So it was almost with a sense of reverence that I placed the bundle in the drawer of the table and locked them safely away.

The burning question was how I was going to extract the information I needed. I realised again the enormity of the task ahead of me, but inside me there was still a fierce sense of purpose about it all. I knew there was little I could do about it that day, so I decided to sleep on it, hoping that a new morning would bring fresh inspiration and intuitions.

I decided that what I needed most was access to some Irish telephone directories. The sister in charge of the adoption agency had told me all those years before that my daughter had been adopted by a medical family. What could be more straightforward than that! All I needed to do was to research medical families in Ireland for the period in question, concentrating on Dublin, the area in which I believed Claire to have been adopted. I felt at this stage that even an up-to-date directory would be a help and of course there was also now the classified directory or *Golden Pages*. I knew from my researches into the address of the adoption agency that my local library had an out-of-date *Eolaí Telefóin na hÉireann* and this would be a start.

I pulled out this same volume (1984 vintage!) and seated myself in the quiet reference room to search the directory for clues. Taking each name in turn on the list of adopters, I tried to match it to a name in the telephone directory, all the time looking for a medical connection. I decided to consider "medical" in the broad sense, looking not just for doctors and consultants but chemists, dentists and opticians. I did not find the information in the *Uiris Oifigiúil* a great help in this quest as, in the main, they used the title "Mr" for all adoptive fathers, irrespective of their occupation. I did actually find the odd medical family that coincided with a name on the list, but the hours ticked by and when the library closed I had to leave it for another day without having made much progress.

It was on the way home in the car that I determined to get hold of old telephone directories from the Department of Posts and Telegraphs in Dublin. If I had them I could do my research at home in my own time. I telephoned the department, only to be informed that directories were not available. They were not in print and only one or two copies were kept for the archives. I could of course see these if I presented myself at their offices in Dublin, but this was of little use to me as many hours— even weeks!—of work would be required.

Suddenly it occurred to me that someone somewhere in Ireland must have the information I needed. I had the brainwave of writing to *The Gay Byrne Show*, Ireland's most popular radio show, which is broadcast five mornings a week. There was a special slot on the programmes which listeners could use to ask for various unusual things, such as out-of-print books, odd rolls of wallpaper no longer commercially available, unusual pieces of china. Why not telephone directories, I thought! It was certainly worth a try.

I wrote to *The Gay Byrne Show* to ask for help, offering in return a donation to the St Vincent de Paul Society. The plan worked. As it happened, I was spending a few days in Hampshire and actually heard the request on the radio. I was sitting in my hotel bedroom over a late breakfast when I heard Gay Byrne say, "Now we have the father and mother of a request! Some poor lady is looking for old telephone directories going back to the late fifties and early sixties. Can anyone possibly imagine what she needs them for? Never mind, we deal with all sorts on this programme and *nothing* ever surprises me these days. She is prepared to give a donation to the St Vincent de Paul Society if anyone can help. Give us a ring on…and do be careful as you climb out of the attic covered in cobwebs!"

All I needed to do now was wait and pray. I was thankful that Gay Byrne had not read out my name and address over the air as some of my Irish relatives would surely have heard and I would have been subjected to all kinds of inquisitions, including discreet and not so discreet enquiries about my sanity.

Two weeks after the broadcast I had a letter from the show, advising me to get in touch with a Mr M Nash, who had said he was willing to help me. Enclosed with the letter was one from this Mr Nash himself to Gay Byrne, telling the broadcaster that he had been trying to get through to the programme for some considerable time without any luck. I thanked God for his perseverance! Not only was he prepared to supply copies of the telephone directory for six of the years in question, but he was prepared to deliver them to me—not realising, of course, that I lived in England.

I wrote back to Michael Nash immediately, enclosing a cheque for postage, and in a matter of days I received the telephone directories. For some time after that Michael Nash and I corresponded. I never met him and after two years I heard no more. I can only assume that he died. He was a lovely man who wanted nothing more than to help someone out, and he never asked me why I wanted the directories. The reason he had them was because his late mother had always believed in keeping everything "just in case it comes in useful some day." In this case the directories certainly did!

CHAPTER TEN

After the initial excitement of receiving the old Irish telephone directories of the sixties and after spending some time looking through them for the names and addresses of old friends, I knew it was time to settle down to some serious research. I had spent every spare minute since their arrival with the directories spread out over the floor of our sitting-room. Goodness knows how I would have explained my occupation to a curious caller! I decided that I needed a private work-room where I could work undisturbed and leave papers and documents on view.

There was a little room on the first floor that I used as a lumber room. In grander days it had been the dressing-room of the master bedroom. I cleared it out, leaving only a chair and a table on which to work. Here I would find peace to do my research to my heart's content. In no time, Michael had dubbed my office the "holy room," and had pinned a notice to the door: "Quiet, please!"

I sifted through the papers containing the names of approximately a thousand children, along with the names and addresses of their adopters—the number adopted in one full year. Female children accounted for about six hundred and fifty. Even at this stage I had no assurance that the child I sought was included in this specific batch but I was determined to keep working at it. Each name I took from the list had to be matched, if possible, with a name and address from the old telephone directory. It was a tedious, painstaking exercise, but I continued until my eyes ached and I had pains in my shoulders from stooping over the table. Sometimes Michael came to give me a hand: I would look up the directory while he made a list of adopters who in some way fitted my idea of a "medical family." It was surprising to discover how many people in Ireland in the sixties had telephones, but how few of these had medical connections. I concentrated— mistakenly, as it turned out—on the Dublin area, feeling that the chances of my daughter having been adopted there were the strongest. Later I discovered that I had been misled, perhaps even deliberately so, by the sister in charge of the adoption agency. It seemed very cruel, when the natural mother has so few memories of her own child, so few straws to grasp at.

As soon as I had begun my research in earnest, I found myself in hospital. I had been feeling a bit unwell for some time but decided that I would ignore my symptoms. I eventually sought medical advice only when I was experiencing quite a bit of discomfort. I presented myself at the doctor's surgery on a Tuesday afternoon. My own GP was on holiday, so I saw another doctor in the practice. After he had examined me, he informed me none too gently that I would need emergency surgery and got in touch with one of the local gynaecological consultants who had a clinic that afternoon in a nearby regional hospital. When I got there he confirmed that I would have a hysterectomy the following day. I was sent home to collect my things and was for admission to hospital at eight that evening. I didn't know whether I was coming or going and have only vague recollections of going around the house muttering, "If anything should happen to me, I want to be buried in Ireland."

By late afternoon of the following day I was back from theatre after a successful operation. It took me a considerable time to recover from the operation and the psychological trauma it entailed. After I was discharged, I had to spend a long period recuperating at home. As I languished in my bed I had plenty of time to think about my life, and about my lost daughter in particular. After the initial period of four weeks' rest, I found myself with plenty of time to tackle further research and, gradually, my energy and concentration returned.

After this crisis, I found that my outlook on life had changed a great deal. Little things that I had previously taken for granted assumed greater importance. Henceforward, I tried to approach each day with a sense of purpose. I realised even more strongly that something central to my life had been taken away all those years before and that I needed badly to reclaim it. So, day in, day out, I continued to peruse the papers I had accumulated. A little voice inside me urged me to go on.

As the weeks after my operation went by I found myself becoming stronger. I was now passing most of my days at a gentle pace, the mornings about the house, the early afternoons having a nap and the late afternoon either visiting a friend or having a friend visit me. As regards my research, I had selected certain names from the *Uiris Oifigiúil* which I considered to be possibilities. This selection was made purely by location (in Dublin) and to a certain extent on gut instinct. I now needed to get birth certificates for the babies I had selected, to verify their dates of birth. The problem I faced was how to get these certificates without arousing suspicion. I was far from the Registry of Births in Dublin and could not repeatedly travel to Dublin from my home for the purpose of collecting these certificates.

I first telephoned the Registry of Births and found out the cost of each certificate; then I took the bull by the horns and wrote, stating my requirements. I had to make the letter as formal as possible without stating *why* I needed the certificates, notwithstanding the fact that such certificates are public documents and are therefore open to anybody to take up. There was only one date of birth in which I was interested, so it was clear to me that someone in the office would get suspicious when they received my request for some ten certificates for babies with different names but the same date of birth! I therefore decided that I would request the certificates one at a time and hope that no connection would be made between the various applications.

Weeks passed and I received no response. Then I received a letter from the Registrar of Births saying that nothing could be found. After this had happened three or four times in response to my requests, I decided to telephone the Registrar's office and ask for assistance. I sat with the telephone in my hand and my heart pounding in my chest. What was I going to do if someone demanded an explanation for my application? I need not have worried—the person I spoke to was extremely nice and helpful. As the conversation went on and I grew more confident, I let it slip that the person for whom the certificate was required had been adopted. My informant in Dublin told me that for such a certificate I need the precise date of the adoption as well as the date of birth.

I was completely flummoxed by this. Where did I go from here? I got in touch with my legal adviser in Dublin, who told me that not only would the adoption agency have the relevant information, but that I was legally entitled to have confirmed for me that my daughter *had* been adopted and also the *date* on which she had been adopted. My morale boosted by this, I wrote to the agency in Dublin and within a matter of ten days they confirmed the date of my daughter's adoption order.

I then wrote again to the Registry of Births, requesting the birth certificates (initially one at a time) and enclosing the relevant fee. In no time at all a steady trickle of certificates was coming through the post. How can I explain how I felt as I waited for the postman each morning to see if any brown envelopes with the official Irish black harps were in his delivery. The post usually arrived around seven, heralded by the barking of my two terriers. I would stumble from my bed, collect the post from the letter-box downstairs, return to bed and sift eagerly through the envelopes. Time went by, but none of the birth certificates that arrived bore the longed-for date of birth. I lived in anticipation, only to have my hopes repeatedly dashed. As the pile of certificates mounted and my bank balance diminished accordingly, I decided that the only thing to do with them was to burn them. They were of no use to me and I felt that, by having them, I was somehow intruding into other people's lives.

On more than one occasion I came very close indeed to the actual date of birth I was searching for. This heightened my conviction that I was on the right track. If children with birth dates very close to Claire's were contained in the lists I had had copied from the *Uiris Oifigiúil*, then I had every reason to suppose that my daughter's adoptive family would be listed in the same pages.

I often wondered what the staff of the Registry of Births thought about this odd woman who was constantly writing to request the birth certificates of different children. Did some compassionate and perceptive person suspect my true motives? In the end, it was all revenue for the Irish government and perfectly legal, so perhaps nobody gave any thought to it.

CHAPTER ELEVEN

On the odd occasion it occurred to me that it would be safer and more efficient to get information by telephone. I was conscious, however, that in order to do this I would have to be very careful indeed not to cause anyone unnecessary distress or to arouse suspicion. The simplest way I could devise to get this information was to pretend to conduct a survey into education and emigration in Ireland with special emphasis on students in the eighteen to twenty-five age group. I would select a name from the list in the *Uiris Oifigiúil*, if possible find the current telephone number of the family in the directory if I could do so and make a call to enquire how many children in the household were in third-level education. After that, I hoped to be able to find out the sex and date of birth of the young people in question, or at least the month and year of birth. I was not particularly proud of having to resort to such tactics but I did feel that this approach was likely to be the least damaging and intrusive of any I could devise. I certainly would not have embarked on such an exercise had I not reached a certain level of desperation in my search for Claire. I must stress that it was on only a few occasions that I resorted to these measures and in general I continued to acquire certificates of birth from the Registry of Births in the normal way.

In May, about three months after my operation, I was waiting at home one afternoon before joining a friend for afternoon tea in her garden. The day was warm for the time of year and I was looking forward to my excursion. I was sitting on the sofa looking at the television when all of a sudden it occurred to me that I should perhaps stop concentrating on adoptive families based in Dublin and widen my area of research. I turned off the television and said a few prayers. I had developed the habit of praying since my illness, especially when I was alone in the house during the day. I appealed to the Almighty for guidance, reminding Him that he had been of precious little help to me so far. I went upstairs to my little work-room, took out the list of adopters in the *Uiris Oifigiúil* and asked God for inspiration. A tall order—but I was very serious about this. I took the list into my bedroom and began to thumb through the pages.

At that moment my eyes focused on a certain name and I was intrigued, as I had already frequently registered this name but had always discounted it on the grounds that the address was outside the Dublin area. I now asked myself: could it possibly be the right name? I had very little to lose by pursuing this line of enquiry so I decided to go for it. I found a telephone number in an old directory, and was able to get the up-to-date number from directory enquiries without any difficulty.

What should I do? I decided there was no time like the

present. I walked into the hall and sat on the chair beside the telephone. I began to dial the number, not at all sure what I would say if someone actually answered. After a few seconds I heard the ringing tone. Just as I was beginning to lose my nerve, the receiver was lifted and a young female voice said hello.

"Hello, is that...?" I asked, giving the number.

"It is," came the reply.

"I wonder if you might be able to help me," I said. "I am doing some research regarding the relationship, if any, between education and emigration from Ireland. It would assist me greatly if you could give me some idea of the number of young people in your family between eighteen and twenty-five. I appreciate that you may not wish to give such information and, if that is the case, I quite understand."

"No, that is all right," came the response. There are two of us in our family in that age-group: John, my brother, who is twenty-two, and I am twenty-three. We have a younger sister, Kate, who is still at secondary school. She is sixteen."

"I'm sorry. I wonder if you could tell me your ages again. Just the year and month in which you were born, that would be fine."

"Well, John was born on — and Kate was born on —. I am Claire and I was born on — December 1964," she replied.

Something like a very sharp pain shot through my body as I realised what this young woman had said. I had, of course, heard her perfectly well, but I had to ask for confirmation. My mouth was dry and my tongue stuck to the roof. In a voice that sounded very faint to me, and one which I hoped did not shake, I gently repeated the question.

"Yes, Claire—may I call you Claire? I have John's date of birth, the month and the year anyway, but I'm not too sure about your own. Would you please give it to me again?"

"Yes," she said. "I was born on — December 1964."

I knew I somehow had to stay calm and end this conversation. I continued to ask what I hoped were appropriate questions regarding education and educational courses. All this time my heart was thumping and my legs were like jelly. I kept shifting position on the chair, my palms were damp with perspiration and I had great difficulty in holding the telephone receiver and the pen with which I was taking notes. I was conscious of Claire's voice telling me about her own education and how she very much hoped that she could remain in Ireland, but as time went on she felt she might have to follow her brother and many of her contemporaries across the sea either to England or the United States.

"I hope you find the type of job you are looking for in Ireland," I concluded. "I feel it's such a shame that young, well-educated people, who have worked so hard at their education, should have to seek work away from Ireland. Claire, can I just thank you very much indeed for all your help? Goodbye, dear, and thanks again."

With that, the line went dead.

I do not know how long I stood in the hall, holding the receiver. I was completely shattered but at the same time exhilarated. Even though it was a warm afternoon, my feet were blocks of ice, as if the circulation had been turned off. I stared and stared at the note-pad in front of me and could not take my eyes off the information I had scribbled down. I kept reading it and reading it over and over until I knew everything I had written by heart. One sentence stood out from the rest: *I am Claire and I was born on — December 1964.*

I eventually moved from the hall into the kitchen. I automatically put the kettle on to make myself a cup of tea, completely forgetting my invitation. My mind was in total turmoil and I could concentrate on nothing. Was I right? Could it really have been Claire? Did I actually speak to the daughter I had given away all those years before? Suddenly it all seemed unreal, as if it was happening to someone else. There was nobody at home but me and my two dogs and I could hardly rely on them for verification of what had happened. As I sat drinking my tea in the kitchen, I continued to mull it over in my mind, my dogs looking expectantly up at me in the hope of getting a biscuit. I was abruptly recalled to reality by the ringing of the telephone.

"Hello," a familiar voice said. "This is Dorothy. Have you forgotten about our arrangement for afternoon tea?" Before I could reply, she asked, "Are you all right?"

I replied that I was fine but that I had indeed forgotten about her invitation.

"I've been trying to reach you on the telephone for the last while but I kept getting the engaged tone."

"Dorothy, I'll be with you in fifteen minutes. I'm sorry you had to telephone to remind me. See you then."

I replaced the receiver and before I could lose myself

in thought again, I put on my jacket to set off on the short walk down the road. As I opened the hall door, I stopped in my tracks, turned around and scribbled a note to Michael for him to find when he came in from school.

> Gone to tea with Dorothy. Back around five.
> Love, Fionnuala.
> PS I think I may have found Claire!

With that, I opened the door again and walked out into the bright May sunshine.

A few minutes later I was sitting in the back garden of Dorothy's house. She had gone off to make the tea, after making sure that I was comfortably installed on a sunbed.

I lay there, looking up at the clear blue sky, all the time thinking about my telephone conversation with Claire. I felt intensely alive, allowing myself to believe that something very significant had taken place. I went over the conversation again and again in my own mind as I tried to picture the young woman at the other end of the line. Was it really *my* Claire? If so, what did she look like? Was she dark like her father, or fair like myself? Whose eyes did she have? Was she tall, or was she small like me? Whose temperament did she have? I allowed these questions to go around and around in my mind for several minutes, then reminded myself that she must be a mixture of the two of us.

Dorothy returned with the tea. I mentally shook myself. I had no guarantee whatsoever that the young woman to whom I had spoken was in fact my daughter. Nevertheless I had the strongest sensation within me that she was. In the meantime, what was the harm in dreaming?

Dorothy remarked on how well I was looking, inviting me to come and take tea. She went indoors again to get some scones she had baked from the oven. As I took a seat at her table, I noticed how beautiful her garden looked. The sun was shining brightly now, and I could feel the warm rays on the backs of my hands. Dorothy's garden was a peaceful place, where I often came to sit and rest; she enjoyed sharing its beauties with her friends. Even now, in May, it looked quite spectacular. The family cat, Guinness, had found his way on to my lap, and was settling himself comfortably in the hope of a titbit.

Looking back on that afternoon, I do not know how I managed to get through it without blurting out my news. It would have caused a sensation, as Dorothy had no idea that I had a daughter in my past. I'm quite sure she would have understood, but at this stage I knew that I had to keep it all to myself. I went through the motions of sensible conversation, although I was very aware of separate thoughts and ideas darting around my own head. The more I thought about the events of earlier that afternoon, the more I began to feel that inside me a little fire had been rekindled.

As soon as I could politely do so, I left Dorothy's house and made my way home. As I rounded the corner of our road, I could see Michael's car parked at the kerb. I quickened my steps and found him in the kitchen, beginning to make supper. I watched him for a few minutes as he busied himself. He had not heard me come in so he looked up in surprise to see me. "I got your note, but I'm afraid I couldn't quite understand it. What's all this about finding Claire?"

I pulled out a chair and sat at the kitchen table. In no time at all I had explained to him what had happened. He was pleased for me but also taken aback. "You never fail to surprise me. Are you sure you know what you're doing? We mustn't jump to conclusions. I know how excited you must be now, but you'll have to give great thought to this."

"I *knew* you'd say that! I *know* how cautious I have to be. I just feel in my bones that this is Claire! There has to be some way of making sure I'm right."

Michael looked at me and could see that I was in a frenzy of excitement. "Let's leave it for now," he said. "After dinner we'll talk about it again. I just hope you're right."

I awoke the next morning with something resembling a hangover—strange, as I had not drunk a drop the evening before. It must have been about ten o'clock. There was nobody about; a mug of cold tea was on the bedside table and the morning post and newspaper were beside me on the pillow.

I managed to make it to the bathroom and felt a little more ready to face the day after a warm shower. I felt that dressing smartly and doing my make-up would give me more confidence to embark on the next phase of my plan.

Much of the drama of the previous afternoon was still with me. Every time I let my mind wander over all that had happened, I was filled with an excitement that was tinged with apprehension. I had to hold on and not allow things to get out of control. I had a very strong sensation of having found my daughter but there was a great deal more to be done before I had conclusive proof.

I knew well what I had to do. There was no other way. I had to get hold of the extract from the register of adopters which would verify the date of adoption, but I knew in my heart that I was far too frightened to do this for myself. What if I made a mess of this crucial part of the procedure? I decided that the solicitor I had consulted in Dublin was my best bet. After all, such solicitors must frequently request these documents for all sorts of reasons: a will, trust matters, or probate.

I sat down and dialled the solicitor's office. He was in court but I managed to speak to his clerk, who was very helpful. She told me that she was going to the Registry within the following few days and could look up the document for me once she had the information she needed. She told me that I should be in possession of the document within the week.

The days went by and I could hardly contain the excitement that bubbled inside me. I was, by now, back at work part-time for a local law firm, so at least my mind was occupied for some of the day. The week passed without a word from Dublin. After about ten days I could restrain myself no longer; I took the bull by the horns and telephoned again. Apparently the person who was to have gone to the Registry was ill but someone else would definitely be there the following day and would take up the relevant document. I got the impression that the person I spoke to found my impatience somewhat surprising, but how could they know how important the whole thing was to me? I had waited a long time for this but my patience had worn very thin by this stage.

In the late afternoon of the following Thursday the telephone rang. The office had the information I had requested. I asked the young woman at the other end of the line to read me out the details of the extract from the register of adopters. I waited in apparent calm as she gave me the name of the child, the address of the adopters and, a vital piece of information, the date of the adoption order. *It was the same as the date I had myself established at the beginning of my search*! I could hardly believe my ears as I mumbled my thanks and asked for the office to send a copy of the document as quickly as possible. I needed physical proof that I had not totally imagined it all.

That afternoon I sat for a long time without doing anything. It seemed as if all my energy had just ebbed away and I was totally exhausted. As I allowed myself to sit quietly in the half-dusk of the evening, my mind wandered over many aspects of my life. Who would ever have dreamed that it would come to this? The more I allowed myself to contemplate the now very real probability that I had actually found my daughter, the more unreal it seemed to become. A nagging doubt would not go away. I knew I was really 99.5 per cent sure, but, I asked myself, what did I need to do to make it 100 per cent? There were to be many ups and downs before I reached that stage of complete certainty.

Subsequently I found that there appeared to be a time for everything and that everything was accomplished in its own time. After each step in the proceedings it seemed natural that I should back off and take a rest, as if nature in some way were keeping me from going too fast. It was a strange feeling, almost as if I needed to hold on to each stage of the search in turn. Only when I felt able to let go of it could I then begin to consider the next step.

And so it was that, having reached this particular milestone, I felt compelled to return to my "normal" life. I had to take care of my husband, house and family on a day-to-day basis. Of course, I had great assistance from Michael, who was with me every step of the way. It was in some sense as if I had two lives, my external one and the internal one that was kept exclusively for me. It would have been nice to express my emotions and share them with close friends, but I really felt that I could not do this. I could only imagine the reaction I would get in somebody's living room over a drink before Sunday lunch if I casually dropped the remark, "I've spent the week heavily engaged in my continuing search for my daughter, who was adopted some twenty-three years ago." A great conversation-stopper!

Chapter Twelve

It was now mid-August and we made the usual plans to go on holiday. Our choice for this year was the West Country; we were to stay in various little places in Devon and possibly Cornwall. In the past we had frequently returned to Ireland for holidays, principally to visit my mother and see other relatives. Now that she had died, there was not the same urgency about family visits and the odd weekend in Dublin during the spring or late autumn filled the bill as far as I was concerned.

Michael was keen to get me away from home to try to take my mind off my continuing search for Claire, if only for a couple of weeks. Things are never that simple! While I packed my bags for my holiday, my brain was full of thoughts, speculation and anticipation regarding Claire. Where I went, there she would also be. I was not in the least obsessive about her, as I had had many years of living with the knowledge of her existence and with the fact of my loss of her. The reactions I had now were much gentler, as the possibility of finding her came closer to reality. It gave me a very warm feeling, a peace I had not known up to this.

It was during our stay in Devon that I decided I would need someone to help with me with the next step in my search. I discussed it a great deal with Michael and we agreed that I had several options open to me. I could, of course, just take up the telephone, tell the girl the truth and hope to God that I was right. That would have been cruel, irresponsible and unforgivable. Anyone with half a wit could imagine the trauma it would cause. I was not the kind of person to take such a course of action. I felt very strongly that if I was to have any success at all in approaching my daughter, I had to do so with sensitivity and honour. After all, I now had a good idea who she was and where she was and could put myself in her shoes. I also had to consider the feelings of her adoptive parents. What might they think about all this? How would I feel if I were in such a position? I was somewhat surprised to realise that a major part of my concern was for the adoptive parents. I had much to consider and I was certain that I needed to be very cautious and very sure of what I was doing.

After my return from Devon, I decided to get in touch with a solicitor in Dublin, I'll call him Frank, who was an old friend of mine and with whom I had formerly worked. We had kept in touch mainly by the exchange of Christmas cards over the years. By now he had a thriving practice in the centre of Dublin. In many ways Frank might have seemed an odd choice to consult on such a matter: he was some years my junior, a bachelor, with no personal experience of the kind of problem I was about to bring to him. What drew me to him was my certain knowledge that he would tell me exactly what he thought and that, if he did decide to go along with my plan, I would be on very firm ground and could rely on him utterly. This appealed to me greatly because it would be so different from the way I had been treated by the adoption agency and their lawyer all those years before. I discussed my plans with Michael and he agreed that I ought to speak to Frank.

When I got through to Frank on the telephone, I found it hard to bring the conversation around to the real reason for my call. I was tongue-tied, something that greatly surprised me. I was simply unable to explain to him in simple English what had happened in the past, my search for Claire and, most important of all, my conviction that I had found her again. Then it dawned on me just how difficult it was for me really to come to terms with all this. Frank, like all my friends and colleagues, had known me without my past and would never have imagined that I had one. It was hardly surprising that I found it difficult to be open about it now, even with someone with whom I felt very secure. After I had tried but failed several times to tell him what was on my mind, we agreed that I should write to him instead and explain what it was that I seemed to be choking upon.

I was annoyed with myself as I put down the telephone. What was he going to think? But I soon realised that I would have to deal with my fear of what people were going to think. It came down, in the end, not to what others thought of me, but to what I thought of myself. The shame and guilt were in the present just as much as they had been in the past. I knew I needed to pull myself together and sort myself out before I went any further. Only when I had accepted myself could I expect others to accept me. I had to put the whole matter in perspective. What had happened in Ireland almost a quarter of a century previously had to be looked at in the light of the present time.

I did manage to sit down and write a letter—quite a long one—to Frank. I found it much easier to explain it all on paper, a facility that I remember having had for essays when I was at school. I wrote to Frank that I needed to approach the matter with extreme caution and to feel great confidence in the person who would support me. After I posted the letter I had a few days to wait for his reply, and waiting is something I am not very good at.

Within a few days the telephone rang and a very robust voice at the other end of the line said, "Is that all?" I was greatly relieved to hear Frank suggest that we should meet and discuss the matter further when he was in England on business. We arranged a meeting for late October. In the meantime he would mull the matter over, make a few discreet enquiries and keep in touch with me.

I was pleased to have an ally such as Frank and knew that my story had grabbed his imagination. I would be happier still if I could convince him to support me in the course of action I had in mind!

The meeting with Frank in London went more or less according to plan. I was delighted to see him again and, after some time spent in catching up on personal and family news, we got down to business. Yes, he would like to help, but needed to know a lot more about the whole affair. He remarked that in all the years he had known me and my family, I had been a dark horse; he would never have suspected that I had been keeping such a secret behind my reserved façade. Now that I had decided to confide in him, he felt he understood me so much better. Nevertheless, he was concerned on two fronts. Did I really know what I was getting myself into? How much did my adopted daughter know about her past—did she even know that she had been adopted? I did my best to allay his concern and gave him copies of the original birth certificate and of the extract from the register of adopters and outlined to him how I had gone about my research. Like any good lawyer, he advised caution and said that things should be taken one step at a time, something I should know well myself. He would make discreet enquiries of a social worker in Dublin and would be in touch.

As Frank waved me a cheery goodbye, I knew I had to be content with that for the time being. The ground rules for our working together had been laid down. In my head I knew his advice was valid; in my heart I felt something else entirely.

One afternoon in February I returned from work to see the little red light flickering on my answering machine in the hall. I left down my bags and switched it on. I heard a thunderous voice on the line saying, "You sound like the Queen! Get yourself over to Dublin by the sixteenth. I have arranged a meeting for you with the agency." One thing for certain was that Frank had not changed over the years!

I telephoned his office in Dublin. He was "in a meeting" but soon I was talking to him. He told me he had telephoned the agency, informing them that a client of his wished to make enquiries about her daughter who had been given up for adoption more than twenty years earlier. Could they help? The person in charge intimated that times had changed and that they would see what they could do. Frank pushed further, suggesting that his client would like to come and see them and asking if an appointment could be arranged. This was apparently no trouble either. He said that he would like to accompany his client at this meeting, if possible. The agency agreed, although the person to whom he was speaking said that it was most unusual, as they normally preferred to see the natural mother alone. It was agreed that Frank would contact me, his client, and confirm the date of the meeting in writing. All that was left was for me to present myself in Dublin on the sixteenth, and Frank and I would approach the agency together. Of course I agreed to everything that he suggested.

I can remember putting down the telephone and being very much aware that I had exactly nine days in which to get my act together. I was on a high, as if the ground was moving under my feet. I mentally made notes of all I would need to do. My one regret was that Michael would not be able to accompany me to Dublin, as he was now well into the school term. Still, I would have Frank there for moral support. I made the necessary flight arrangements and organised my home and work duties to facilitate my journey. Last but not least, I had to work out how to present myself to the agency. I ran upstairs to examine my wardrobe. Did I have anything suitable to wear? What would be "appropriate" clothes for the occasion?

By the time Michael arrived home I was in a spin of organisation. Eventually he managed to sit me down and get me to talk things over in a quiet and sensible way, but I could see that he was just as excited as I was and delighted at my news.

It was a very tired woman who thanked God before going to sleep that night.

CHAPTER THIRTEEN

I was thankful that Aer Lingus Flight EI 159 would soon be landing at Dublin Airport. I was not the bravest of travellers and being on my own tended to make me all the more nervous. I was very pleased that my cousin Lucy would be meeting me at the airport.

I folded away my newspaper and sat back in my seat, all the while looking out the window at the fields and houses increasing in size as we floated downwards. Holding my breath slightly, I waited for the inevitable bump which comes with touchdown and then I allowed myself to relax, safe in the knowledge that we had landed.

Lucy was waiting for me. I was going to spend the night with her and would meet up with Frank the following day. It was early evening, so we went out together for a meal in an nearby hotel. Lucy was amazed when I put her in the picture. She had no previous knowledge of Claire, or of the events of the past. Once she got over the initial shock, she was very supportive. I had often stayed with Lucy when I came over to Dublin to ɔend a weekend, so she had not suspected that this trip was to be any different.

The following morning I was awake before the alarm went off. I had not slept at all well and when I awoke I felt as if someone had hit me on the head with a sledge-hammer! I was grateful when I saw Lucy's arm appear around the bedroom door with a mug of hot tea.

I sat in bed for a very long time after she had gone to work. I was not meeting Frank until half-past two in the afternoon, and the appointment with the agency was at four. I had, it seemed, all the time in the world to think about it. Having listened to *The Gay Byrne Show* on the radio for some time, I decided it was time to take a shower and get dressed. I had planned my wardrobe prior to coming to Dublin, so it was not too arduous a task to slip into the slate-grey suit I had thought appropriate for the interview at the agency.

On the way into town I decided I really ought to get my hair done. As well as making me feel better, it would help to fill in the time. Under normal circumstances I would have had no trouble in passing time in Dublin, but that day I knew I could not concentrate very well on anything other than my immediate plans. As I walked along Grafton Street, looking for a hair salon, I suddenly remembered that it was Ash Wednesday and made my way into Clarendon Street Church for Mass. It was thronged with people and I watched the faces of the women as they prayed, marvelling at the burdens carried so uncomplainingly by so many wives and mothers.

I was jolted back to reality by the buzzer on someone's watch and soon exchanged the smell of burning candles and the whispered prayers of the faithful for the aroma of ground coffee and the loud chatter of Bewley's Café, where I had lunch.

Only a few doors away I found the hair salon that had been recommended to me by Lucy earlier that morning. It was a wonder I even remembered the name. Normally I enjoy having my hair done but today I really felt I could not be bothered with any form of conversation. The young woman who was doing my hair asked the usual questions: "Are you going somewhere nice this evening? Is the hair-do for a special occasion?" I had great difficulty in giving her truthful answers without leaving myself in the position of having to amplify my responses. It was, of course, a very special occasion, but how could I tell her that?

At a quarter to three I was walking along Grafton Street, knowing I was late for my appointment. Apart from the discourtesy, I was keen not to get on the wrong side of Frank who, after all, was going out of his way to help me. I practically raced along Dame Street, reminding myself to be careful not to fall. I had no desire to enter the agency with bloody knees and laddered tights. What an impression that would have created! I needed to arrive there looking as if I was totally in control.

As I expected, Frank was waiting for me. I was surprised to see him casually dressed, looking not at all like somebody about to go to an important meeting. He greeted me affably, although muttering under his breath about women and time. He asked if I wanted some tea or coffee, both of which I refused. He then offered gin or whiskey, which I again declined. As a last resort, he enquired if I would like some Valium, which, yet again,

I declined. He gently reminded me that I was thirty minutes late and said he had begun to wonder just where the hell I was!

We discussed various aspects of the forthcoming meeting and went over the relevant papers to be sure we understood each other. At this stage I got very agitated. I felt that if we did not hurry we would be late for the appointment. Frank told me that he had had a copy of the birth certificate and extract from the register of adopters delivered by hand the previous afternoon, so the agency would already be in possession of those. Then he took himself off to change into his city suit. I was left alone to wait. I paced the floor for quite a time, occasionally looking out through the long windows of the room into the street below. The traffic was beginning to build up now and I watched it as it snaked its way along, feeling greater and greater panic as I convinced myself that we couldn't possibly get to the agency on time. My greatest fear was that the appointment would have to be cancelled, making my trip to Dublin a waste of time.

I need not have worried. I had forgotten how fast and skilful Frank was when he got behind the wheel of a car. By this time, in any case, I was too worried about our appointment to care what happened in the car, so I just held on tight and hoped we would arrive in one piece. We pulled up at the kerbside outside the agency with seconds to spare.

Frank had something of a reputation for being "a hard man" and he tended to be sparing with words of sympathy, so I was somewhat surprised to hear him ask, "Are you all right, Fionnuala?" as we got out of the car. Walking up the long, narrow flight of steps to the hall door, I watched him out of the corner of my eye. He was looking straight ahead with a very inscrutable expression. As he heaved open the heavy wooden door I pulled my coat tighter around my shoulders and braced myself for whatever I was to encounter inside.

A young woman in the reception area greeted us cordially enough. The sister in charge would, it seemed, see us in a few minutes. She showed us into a little room and asked us to wait. Once the door closed behind her I became very restless, standing up and walking about the room and looking at the pictures on the wall. I can remember tucking my hands into my pockets as I suddenly began to feel very cold. Just then my eye fell on a small picture with a verse written underneath. I recall that it was about the blessings of adoption and how enriching it could be to welcome a child into your home. It made me conscious how little attention had been paid to *my* trauma when I had to give my baby up for adoption—and I was sure that the same was true for single mothers right up to the present day. I was just about to launch into a tirade, but Frank gently but firmly advised me to calm down. He reminded me that we had come there together for a purpose and that there was little point, after having travelled so far along the road, in my blowing it all now by losing my cool. Of course, he was right. I sat down again on one of the hard chairs.

After what seemed like an eternity, but in reality was only about ten minutes, we were joined by the sister in charge. She was a woman of slight build, in her late fifties, in the garb of a religious. She appeared to be a bit nervous and agitated, coming towards us to shake hands before sitting herself down and placing a brown manilla file on the table in front of her. Once the pleasantries were disposed of, Frank explained the the reason for our visit. All the time he was speaking I was looking at the file on the table. I presumed that it was my file and that it contained the information that I so desperately needed to confirm my own findings. It occurred to me to make a grab for the file and run, but almost as soon as I considered doing this, I banished the idea. After all, I had come there to show them that I was a caring and responsible woman, whose only desire was to seek out her daughter in the least traumatic way possible for the girl. All the years of searching would be rendered futile by one reckless act. I decided that the only possible way for me to get what I wanted was to play by the rules—to say nothing of how Frank would have reacted if I had behaved so foolishly.

I did take a very active part in the conversation but I cannot remember most of what I said. Frank told the sister that he had known my family for many years, that we had discussed matters at very great length and that, having exhausted every avenue of argument and persuasion, he felt that my decision to pursue the search to the end was now inevitable. The sister replied that, with regard to the documentation that Frank had presented, the agency could not confirm or deny its validity, or indeed make any comment about it. She reminded us that the agency operated according to the strictest rules of confidentiality and that such rules could not be broken. I remember that she asked me about my stay in Dublin and when I would return to the UK. It seemed that she could not wait to see the back of me, but I could understand this, really. After all, here I was, nothing but a thorn in her side.

Just before we left I asked whether the adoptive parents were aware of the enquiries I had made and I was told that they were. I then requested that a photograph of myself and a short letter about myself be passed to my daughter. The sister did agree to this, but said she could not guarantee when it would be given to her. Seeing my great disappointment, she assured me that she would, as soon as possible, be in contact with the adoptive mother. But she reminded me that I had no legal rights whatsoever. I had to accept what she said, but it was only with difficulty that I prevented myself from replying that perhaps I had some moral rights.

When the interview was finished, Frank and I walked down the highly-polished linoleum stairs. I tried to sort out the events of the afternoon in my mind. Almost with a sense of desperation, I turned to Frank and said, "We *are* right, Frank, aren't we?" He thought for a minute before replying, "Yes, Fionnuala, we are right." Not another word was spoken until we got into the car and shut the doors. I was keen to be off as quickly as possible, as I was sure that someone was watching us from behind the curtains. Frank, on the other hand, seemed to need to catch his breath for a few minutes before he started the engine and we pulled away from the kerb. We drove back to his office in almost complete silence. I was both mentally and physically exhausted and my companion seemed to be deeply preoccupied.

Once back at the office, Frank took himself off to sign letters for the post and I went into the conference room to wait. I wanted to telephone Michael to let him know how things had gone and I desperately needed a little time to myself, but I was nonetheless grateful to be interrupted by Anne, Frank's office manager, who kindly brought me a cup of strong tea. We chatted for some minutes, Anne intimating that Frank considered the outcome of the meeting to be "hopeful." I said I was convinced that I was right about Claire; why else would the nun have asked me when I was going back to England? She seemed to be in a great hurry to see me out of the country.

That evening Frank and I went out to dinner and discussed our next move. He was optimistic but felt that we should let the dust settle before we tried to do anything further. Somewhere between the main course and the coffee we agreed that we would wait for about four to six weeks before asking further questions. The plan then was to enlist the help of the agency in arranging a meeting between Claire and myself. Both of us felt it better to go through the proper channels, meanwhile continuing to behave responsibly. All I wanted was to see my daughter and I wished to bring this meeting about with the minimum of trauma and anxiety not only for her but for her adoptive parents. That was the whole point of asking assistance from the agency.

It was a tired and bewildered woman who left Dublin the following day. I was anxious to be back with my own family. I felt I needed, above all else, the security and companionship which only Michael could give me. I had come a long way by visiting the agency with Frank and I hoped that wheels would now be set in motion. My daughter would know that her natural mother was serious about her search for her and, more importantly, that her mother was a responsible, if somewhat desperate, woman.

CHAPTER FOURTEEN

Life went on its merry way for some weeks after my return to England. I was tired and emotionally drained and therefore content to let things ride, at least for the first few weeks. After that I became restless and keen once more to poke my finger in the pie to see what else I could find there.

I was fortunate in that my job at a firm of solicitors involved me a good deal in court work. This really was my safety net as I could channel my energy into worrying about other people rather than myself. Frank, for his part, wrote to me from time to time to keep tabs on me. There were occasions when I would telephone him in desperation to ask if there had been any news from the agency and it was not at all unusual for us to have a bit of an argument on the telephone. Easter came and went and I received a letter from Frank telling me that the agency had written to him to say they would pass a letter on to Claire if I wanted them to do so. This, of course, was a huge breakthrough and obviously this initiative had to have come from her. I was over the moon. At least I knew now that she had been told of my existence and that contact with the adoptive family had been established.

Once I got over the initial excitement, I began to panic! How do you even begin to write such a letter? What on earth do you say? How can you sort out all the jumble of feelings built up in one maternal heart over so many years and commit those feelings to paper? It seemed that this letter was going to take time to write and need a great number of drafts and revisions. Frank, in his wisdom, suggested that I start by writing a very long letter, putting down all my thoughts and feelings, and that when I felt I had included everything I wanted to say, I could then edit it, leaving in what I felt to be necessary and discarding the remainder. In some ways that felt like a rather clinical means of going about it, but in the end I took his advice and spent many hours writing and rewriting in the hope that in the end I would feel happy with what I had done. It was still a labour of great love, and in writing I found a certain peace and satisfaction that I was at last able actually to communicate with my daughter, albeit on paper.

What kind of stationery to use for such an important letter? I was to spend many hours in stationery shops selecting various types of paper, only to reject them and start all over again. In the end, I decided on champagne-coloured paper and matching envelopes. The letter itself would need to be hand-written. It would, I felt, be the height of rudeness to type it. I do not have particularly good handwriting and this also worried me as I had been brought up in an era when the quality of handwriting was thought to reveal a great deal about the writer. After all, this was to be my introduction to Claire, and for ages I agonised over the presentation of the letter. It all seems very silly now, as I am sure the fact of the letter and its contents were the only things that mattered to her. When finally I had satisfied myself that I could not do any better, I gave myself permission to send it off. It was enclosed with a cover letter in a larger envelope and addressed to the agency. I left the letter to Claire open so that the staff of the agency could read it if they wished.

I was to wait many weeks for a response. During this period, I was told by someone that Barnardos in Dublin had a counselling telephone line which was open on a certain afternoon each week. It was intended primarily for young people who wanted advice about seeking their natural parents. I was desperate for anything that would help. One afternoon, after many attempts, I managed to get through. I explained my situation to a social worker and she was very understanding indeed. I had to disclose only my first name and the nature of my enquiry. I needed to know something of what young people felt about their natural mother apparently abandoning them by giving them up for adoption. I was convinced that they must feel totally rejected and—understandably— bitter towards their natural mother. I was surprised to learn that most young people understood that there was a valid reason for mothers having to take such a drastic step. I was, naturally, very heartened by this news. The social worker also advised me to take up Claire's original birth certificate, something I had not considered doing before this. I knew that the certificate existed but did not realise that there would be something therapeutic about actually holding it in my hand and reading it for myself. When I received it from the Registry of Births, I felt that another piece of the jigsaw was in place and that physically holding the document helped me to "own" what had happened all those years ago. I did have a daughter; she really did exist!

Just before we went on our summer holidays to stay with friends in Switzerland, I received a short letter from the agency to say that Claire had been in touch by telephone and that she wanted to meet me. It is impossible to describe how I felt. I was standing in the hall, having put the phone down after speaking to Frank, when the afternoon post arrived. My two terriers, little terrors that they are, rushed for the letter-box and were about to set upon the envelope that lay on the mat when I bounded forward and retrieved it. I took the crumpled envelope in my hands and registered the Dublin postmark. It was with my heart pounding in my chest that I tore it open to see four or five lines of type on a sheet of white paper. Apparently, on the Friday afternoon of the previous week, Claire had telephoned the agency to say she wished to make contact with her mother. I really could not believe it. I read the letter over and over, put it back into the envelope and placed it in my pocket, only to take it out and read it several times again to satisfy myself that it really was happening. By the time Michael arrived home a couple of hours later, I was practically walking on the ceiling with excitement.

Over a cup of tea in the kitchen I talked the whole thing over with Michael. He was, naturally, very pleased for me, and immediately arranged to take me out to dinner as he wanted to celebrate. On a more practical level, I am sure he felt I would not be safe around the pots and pans in the kitchen, so for all our sakes eating out was the only solution that night! Later that evening I telephoned Frank in Dublin and he, too, felt this was a great advance. He told me I was "wonderful," which was in sharp contrast to some of the things he had called me over the previous months!

The following morning I telephoned the agency myself and spoke to the sister in charge. She assured me that Claire had been in touch and that I could now be confident that "it was all going to happen." There would, of course, have to be a meeting between the agency and Claire, to make sure that Claire really wanted to go ahead with the meeting and for her to be counselled prior to that meeting if necessary. This meant that there would be some delay before we could meet. The agency would be in touch in two or three weeks to bring me up to date and to let me know when I could expect a meeting.

It all seemed so positive that I felt I could afford to wait the few weeks in order to allow Claire to adjust to the idea of meeting me. I was aware also that I needed time to prepare for such an important meeting. I was positively over the moon and ran up the stairs, two steps at a time, singing "The Kerry Dances" at the top of my voice. It was a warm summer's day and the windows of the house were thrown wide open, so the neighbours could be forgiven for thinking that they lived next door to a lunatic. I was not unduly worried—after all, it is not every day that a natural mother hears that her daughter wishes to make contact with her.

I immediately began to plan my trip to Ireland. There was so much to arrange that for days on end I could concentrate on hardly anything else. I knew, of course, that we were committed to a holiday in Switzerland; our journey had been booked and our friends were expecting us. I hoped that the meeting with Claire would come before then. That was not to happen. Little did I realise at the time just how long I would have to wait; nor indeed could I have anticipated the problems and set-backs that were in store for me.

Very shortly after Claire had made contact with the agency, everything, it seemed, ground to a halt. I was trying to be objective and patient, but as the weeks passed and nothing happened, the tension within me grew. What was going on? I telephoned the agency on average about once every two weeks, only to be told that they had heard nothing further from Claire. As the weeks turned into months, I had to come to terms with the possibility that she had changed her mind. Perhaps she had taken fright, realised the enormity of the step she was about to take and decided not to pursue the matter further. What I found hardest of all to cope with was the ominous silence on Claire's part. The agency wrote to her but received no reply. When I discovered this, I was distraught, as there was no reason for it. The agency staff were sympathetic, but obviously could not force matters in any way, as they were merely acting as go-betweens for the two parties.

Eventually, Claire did get in touch with the agency by letter to ask that she be given my full name and address. She wanted to write to me directly, or so it seemed. It was now up to me to decide what I wanted to do. I would have to write a formal letter to the agency, giving them permission to release details about me. I hesitated for a short time, finding it hard to understand why Claire was not going about things in the normal manner. I hoped that she would understand that I was cooperating with the agency with the best possible intentions. Releasing my name and full address was, of course, an affirmation of my confidence in her and I very much hoped that she would see this to be so. Above all else, I hoped that now, at last, she would feel secure enough to make the vital move to arrange a meeting with me. I could only wait and see.

CHAPTER FIFTEEN

Before I knew it, I was on board a British Airways flight to Zurich for my summer holidays. I kept telling myself that only a lunatic would fail to feel excited at the prospect of two weeks in Switzerland. For Michael's sake, I had to put the best face I could on it, but I was feeling great restlessness and turmoil. We were staying with friends in a beautiful apartment in Verbier, high up in the Alps. The weather was warm and sunny and a lot of our time was spent either sightseeing or walking in the mountains. I recall many a lovely evening after supper, sitting on the balcony listening to Mozart, watching the sunset and wondering what was going to happen when I returned to England.

In late August we returned home. Absolutely no news! I was shattered, and began seriously to consider forcing the issue. My patience was running out. I was so desperate that I even began to consider the possibility of engaging private investigators, but no sooner had this idea occurred to me than I realised it would be a crazy step. I was, without doubt, a woman tormented by my enforced inertia, although on the surface I appeared to be functioning normally and did my best to look after my job, my husband and my home.

Sometimes in the evenings before I went to bed, the telephone would ring and then stop. At other times, when I answered it, there appeared to be nobody there. I often wondered if it might be Claire. By late October I felt I couldn't take any more and once again wrote to Claire, *via* the agency. After all, I was supposed not to know where she was. I told her as gently as I could that my patience was running out and that I could not wait forever for a response from her. At this stage I felt that any response would be better than none, even a note saying that she didn't want to see me. After two further weeks of waiting I decided I could not stand the tension any longer. I telephoned Aer Lingus and booked a flight for ten days later. The die was now cast. I had no intention of telling Frank what my plan was; after all, he might try to stop me!

I arrived at Dublin Airport and my cousin Lucy met me. We went out for a meal and I told her what I intended to do. I asked her if she would help me, as I would feel a lot happier if somebody else was doing the driving. She immediately agreed. We left Dublin for the south the next morning. I had decided to collect some flowers on the way. The previous evening I had spoken to Lucy about this, saying that I wanted a basket of pink and white roses, carnations and freesias. I was surprised the next morning when I walked into the flower shop, to see on display just what I wanted, sitting there waiting for me! We put the flowers in the back of the car and headed for the country, stopping off for lunch at a little town *en route*. By now, Lucy was getting anxious about what I was going to do.

In the afternoon we arrived at our destination and located the house without too much difficulty. There was no sign of life at all, so we found a hotel and waited there. Meanwhile I wrote on the card which the florist had given me to put with the flowers: "Claire, I have arrived. I would love to meet you. Will telephone later if you are not at home when these are delivered."

We sat on two bar stools, like two old women, talking about everything under the sun. In the end, Lucy asked me what I was going to do. She was wonderful; she did not push me or rush me into anything. It must be borne in mind that we were not at all sure that we would find Claire at home when we called or, for that matter, certain that Claire was the person I believed her to be. I had done my research and everything within me told me I was right, but soon we would know for sure. I remember quite clearly saying to Lucy that I would go to the house when it began to get dark. I have, to this day, no idea why I chose that time; perhaps I hoped that twilight would help me to approach the house unnoticed.

At around four o'clock we drove to the house. It was now dusk and lights could be seen from the road. As we approached we noticed a car parked in the drive. At least somebody was at home! Could it, would it, possibly be Claire?

I stared at the house and tried to control the torrent of pent up feelings within me. This was it. I felt I was on the edge of a volcano. Through the gate I could see the tarmac driveway. I estimated the walk to be about twenty yards.

I said to Lucy, "I'm going now. Will you please give me the key to open the boot." Lucy placed the key on the palm of my quivering hand. I stepped out of the vehicle into the soft evening air. Rain had been falling for some time and the road was wet. As I walked to the back of the car I had to side-step a big puddle. I fumbled about with the key, eventually got it into the lock and opened the boot. Before removing the flowers, I tried to place the card in the holder on the arrangement, but my hands were shaking so much that I could not do so. In the end I placed the flowers on the ground and, stooping down, used both hands to insert the card into the holder. I straightened myself up and without a backward glance walked slowly towards the front door. I must have seemed a lonely figure coming out of the darkness into the light of the porch. I clearly recall how I felt at that minute, knowing that there was now no turning back. I looked at the stout, heavy-timbered door and my right hand reached for the knocker. I was barely conscious of the clanging noise of metal upon metal.

I stood in silence for a few seconds before I heard footsteps coming towards me. The door opened and there before me stood a man in his sixties, tall and of thin build. Our eyes met as we appraised each other and his glance fell on the basket of flowers. There was no hint of recognition on his face.

"Good evening," I managed to say. "I wonder if Claire is at home."

"She is," he replied.

"I would like to see her for a few moments if I may," I continued. All the time my eyes were searching his face for any hint of recognition. After all, I reminded myself, he ought to have the advantage over me, as my photograph had been sent to Claire and he must have seen it.

"Would you like to step in out of the cold evening?" he courteously asked. "I'll go and get her for you."

I stepped on to the mat, just inside the door, and watched him walk down the hall. I was now all alone in a well of silence as I stood and waited for something to happen.

I did not have to wait too long before the door at the bottom of the hallway opened and a young woman of slight build with fair hair was walking towards me. As our eyes met, she smiled at me and said, "You must be Fionnuala." In that split second I knew I had been right all along. I remember looking at her and saying, "I'm sorry, Claire; I just had to come." She smiled again and, pushing open a door into a small room, said, "Let's go in here where we can sit and talk."

As we sat down together to talk that afternoon, there appeared to be a great normality about it all. Yet the situation was unreal, so unreal that I could hardly take in what was actually happening. As I looked at this very pretty young woman I found it almost impossible to believe that she was my daughter. I recall being totally mesmerised by this person who moved, spoke and smiled. I kept wanting, yet was afraid, to reach out and touch Claire so as to convince myself that she was actually there and would not disappear again like some ghost or shadow from the past. I remember searching her face for some similarity to mine, then deciding she was not like me at all and that I could quite easily have passed her in the street without a second glance. I expect she was also searching my face for some likeness, something to link us together.

After a short time, the adoptive father, Ed, came into the room, ostensibly to check that the central heating had come on. Claire introduced us and he was friendly and welcoming. He left us again almost immediately, no doubt satisfied that all was well, and as I continued my conversation with my long-lost child I could only marvel at how natural it all seemed—like two old friends talking together. The chat mainly concerned me and my life since Claire's birth and her life, what she was doing now and hoped to do in the future.

Fifteen or twenty minutes later the door opened again and Maura, the adoptive mother, appeared carrying a tray with a welcome cup of tea. It must have been a difficult experience for her to come face to face with Claire's natural mother. I remember standing up when she came in; after all, I was an uninvited visitor to her house. She was a woman in her mid-fifties and the first thing I noticed was the warmth of her smile. She put the tray down, clasped both my hands and said to me, "Fionnuala, you are very welcome in this house. I know you may find that hard to believe, but it is true. We are *so* pleased to meet you at last." I was a bit taken aback by her words, but marvelled at her presence of mind and her ability to act in such a Christian way. I felt she truly meant what she said. She was about to leave us when I said I hoped that she would join us for a chat. With that, all three of us sat down together around the hearth, in which a coal-effect fire was now glowing. We discussed the whole business and how each of us had felt. It was such an extraordinary experience but, again, seemed the most natural thing in the world.

Maura eventually left us to go into the village, warning the two of us to "be good" until she got back. Turning to me, she said, "Fionnuala, I am not going until I get a hug." We embraced. Opening the door to go, she made a remark about the weather and asked about our journey from Dublin. I said we had made very good time and then suddenly remembered that Lucy was still outside in the car. Maura went out immediately and brought her in. I was admonished for my lack of consideration but I felt somehow that under the circumstances Lucy would forgive me .

Lucy was very surprised to see how calm I appeared when she walked into the room and saw Claire and me together. She did, however, immediately notice certain similarities between us: in particular that Claire used her eyes in the same expressive way as I did. We were also about the same height. Later, I realised that Claire had my small hands and that we took the same small shoe size.

Maura returned to take us in to supper in the kitchen. She remarked on the way that she had thought of setting the table in the dining-room but then considered the kitchen to be more appropriate as "after all, we are family here." As we sat around the kitchen table, we chatted about this and that, but at the same time I could observe Claire across the table from me. I tried to keep my eyes on her while responding politely to the rest of the company.

Lucy and I left the house immediately after supper, as I felt that the invasion had gone on long enough. It was now very dark outside and we had a long journey ahead of us. Claire stood out on the driveway to say goodbye. As we hugged each other, I told her to go inside out of the cold. It seemed the most natural thing to say. She, however, had other ideas, and remained on the driveway to watch the car pull away.

As we made our way towards Dublin, Lucy told me that she had felt afraid for me as I approached the house. She said she could not bear to look, and that in the end she moved the car back down the road so that she could sit and wait out of view. On the way back to Dublin, exhaustion overcame me, and I hardly spoke at all. I sat in the warmth of the car, all the time hugging the realisation that Claire and I had at last met, that it *really had happened* and that things had not gone too badly at all. Lucy wisely left me to my own thoughts.

Once back at Lucy's house I telephoned Michael, who had been waiting all day for news, worrying just what his wife was up to. He was greatly relieved when I told him that I had met Claire and that Lucy and I had had tea with her and her family.

I don't remember much of the evening after that, except that Lucy and I sat down to look at the late news and decided afterwards that we wanted nothing more to eat than a bowl of muesli and a cup of tea. I knew in my heart that sleep would be a very long time in coming. In the end, I read all of the *Irish Times* before finally putting the light out at half-past two. Sometime before dawn, sleep eventually came.

Next morning Lucy said, "Fionnuala, I don't know if you realise it, but you've been going around the house for some time with a permanent smile on your face."

I looked at her and said, "And why wouldn't I have? After all, I really have something to smile about now."

With that she hugged me.

CHAPTER SIXTEEN

Despite all the excitement of my trip to Ireland, I was very pleased to be back home again. Michael and I had a great deal to talk about and for many a night afterwards it was well into the small hours before we got to sleep.

About a week after my return I received a letter from Claire, thanking me for my visit. This, of course, was a source of special joy for me and I felt gratitude towards all those who had helped to make it possible.

For a long time I was unable to talk frankly to anyone other than Michael about what had taken place in Ireland. I felt I had to keep everything inside me; if I let go, I might find it all disappearing into thin air!

The first Christmas after meeting Claire I spent hours on end just talking to Michael about her, as if, somehow, this would make her more real. When flowers arrived from Claire for my birthday in December, followed by her Christmas card, I was beside myself with joy, which seemed to manifest itself as floods of tears! With this release came a great peace, and it was a happy woman who went to midnight Mass on Christmas Eve.

Early in the new year I felt that my son, Rory, had a right to know what his mother had been up to. He must have wondered why I was so frequently making trips to Ireland, but no doubt reasoned that I would explain that to him in my own time. He arrived home one afternoon in February with his fiancée, Christine. I decided the time was right so I told him I needed to speak to him privately. As gently as possible, I put him in the picture. When he had time to catch his breath, he sat on the side of the bed with me and said, "I understand about these things. It must have been very difficult for you." I was moved by these words of wisdom coming from someone so young. Once he had got over his initial surprise at the revelation, he wanted to know everything about Claire.

My brother, Michael, was the next one on my list and I certainly was not looking forward to the prospect of telling him. A week or so before Easter I took the bull by the horns and wrote him a long letter. I was deeply concerned about what his reaction would be. He was my only brother and the only surviving member of my immediate family. Perhaps I expected him to respond in the same way as my own parents had responded all those years ago. The letter lay on the hall table for over a week before Michael took the decision to post it for me! Once I knew the letter had been sent, I felt the matter was out of my hands, but it did not prevent me from jumping each time the telephone rang.

On Good Friday afternoon, just after we came back from church, the call came. I answered it myself, so there was no escape. I need not have worried myself: Michael was delighted for me, although he said, "You certainly know how to take the wind out of somebody's sails!" He said he was going to wait until after Easter to write to me, but his wife, Carmel, insisted that he telephone me as she knew how worried I would be. She also told him that she would have wanted to do exactly the same thing if she were in my shoes. There were, naturally, a few tears shed during the phone call, but I felt that the conversation strengthened a relationship that had weakened over the years, due in part to my inability to speak about Claire, and my brother's reluctance to persuade me to do so. I could now openly talk about her to my sister-in-law and to my niece and nephews. It was a great relief, and the younger generation seemed to take it all in their stride. How times change!

Next on my list were our very good friends, Mary and George. We had been close for a long time, although they were somewhat older than Michael and me. We went to lunch with them and I told Michael that I felt they ought to know. We had shared a number of our experiences and had been part of the same prayer group in our community for many years.

After lunch, as we had coffee, Michael said that I had something to tell them. There was complete silence after I had finished my story. I had been so involved in the telling of it that I did not notice the concentration on the faces of my two friends. When I looked at Mary I could see tears cascading down her face, as she said, "Fionnuala, it's a wonderful story, but, oh, how you must have suffered." George was also deeply moved and said it was the best news he'd heard for ten years. Before we left that afternoon, Mary remarked on how gently I had told the story and how she sensed a new peace in me.

We felt also that Michael's parents ought to know. Again I was greatly heartened by their reaction. They were surprised to hear what had happened to me, as they had had no inkling of it. Nevertheless, they could share my joy and they were very anxious to see photos of Claire.

I cannot finish this chapter without paying tribute to my GP, Jon Chappell, who has been a great source of comfort and inspiration to me. Once he knew that I had finally made up my mind to search for Claire, I think he felt a mixture of relief that I had reached a decision and apprehension as to what the outcome would be and how this could affect me. The afternoon I went to see him and told him that I had decided to go to Ireland to see if I could call on Claire, I remember saying to him with desperation in my voice, "I will go to Ireland and I will get what I want." Looking back on them now, those words could be taken for pure selfishness on my part, but Jon Chappell knew otherwise. He looked at me for a few minutes in silence, and then said, "I very much hope you will, Fionnuala. I feel it has come to a stage where you must see this out to the end. I wish you luck."

Claire and I keep in regular touch. We do this mainly by letter but we also communicate by telephone, especially if there is something important to convey. We spend time together, usually long weekends when we both can unwind and catch up on each other's news.

It is wonderful for me to be able to count Claire as part of my family. An example of this is my joy at being able to go into a shop and come upon something that I know would suit Claire. It really is the little things that give the most pleasure: perhaps an unexpected letter arriving or sending flowers. It is wonderful simply being able to acknowledge that I have a child and being able to communicate with her.

Epilogue

Looking back on my life over the past five or six years, I can see an enormous transformation. I am a different person now, more alive and certainly more in touch with myself.

For me to know over the years that something was wrong in my life without being able to do anything about it was very frustrating. Working with a therapist to unravel some of the "knots" in my life, understanding how certain experiences had affected me in various ways was a source of great solace to me, but I came to a watershed and realised that the root of my problems was the loss of my child more than a quarter of a century before. There was great healing in the search for Claire itself; though at times I really felt it was more trouble than it was worth, something always drove me to continue.

To find Claire in such happy circumstances, knowing that she had a good life with people who loved her—that was my dream come true and in itself an answer to prayer.

I am very proud of her, and of her loyalty and dedication to her adoptive parents. I feel no resentment whatsoever towards her adoptive mother, something which surprised me greatly. I am sure that the warmth and welcome extended to me by Maura contributed to this. The secret was that we all wanted what was best for Claire. I can never reclaim the quarter of a century I spent without my child, and the loss of those years is not made any easier to bear by the knowledge that I had little choice in the matter. I think, however, that it is futile to waste time dwelling on the past when I can make the very best of the present and the future.

Although Claire is my child, she is Maura's daughter and I would not want that any other way. I did not decide to reenter Claire's life in the hope of taking her away from her family; that would have been an exercise both foolish and futile. Had that been the result, I would undoubtedly have destroyed everything I hoped for when I set out on my quest. I wanted to find a happy, loved, well-adjusted person and that is what I did find.

Claire must still feel a certain ambivalence about some things and that is a matter for her and me alone. It will take time to build a lasting relationship between us but with effort on both sides it will be possible. We are already good friends and we have made an excellent start.

I have no specific advice to give to anyone tempted to embark on a search such as mine. Each case is different and each natural mother's circumstances are unique. I achieved what I did after a lengthy period of soul-searching, sometimes indescribable frustration and only because of a steely determination to succeed. There never was the remotest guarantee of success. My personal life is greatly enriched by my new relationship with Claire, but at times during the search, I was under enormous stress. I owe a great debt of gratitude to my husband, Michael, without whom I could never have managed. As a result of all this I feel that my understanding of human nature and human frailty has been greatly enhanced.